Presents

Yvette Richard's
Single Black
Female

Published by
THE X PRESS, 55 BROADWAY MARKET, LONDON E8 4PH.
TEL: 081 985 0797

Distributed by Turnaround, 27 Horsell Road, London N5 1XL
Tel: 071 609 7836

Printed by BPC Paperbacks Ltd, Aylesbury, Bucks.

For all women who know
that love, 'still lives here'.

MAN'S BEST FRIEND

"It's just a dick *thang*, you wouldn't understand..."

Breaking up amicably wasn't good enough for my last steady man Troy, he had to be cruel. After nine months together, he summed up all our relationship meant to him in those five little words, because he knew it would hurt me. It was Thanksgiving and I had invited him to dinner at Luigi's, not far from my lakeshore apartment in Chicago. The relationship was finished, worn out and burned out, but I still wanted to stay friends. That's not Troy's style. No woman had ever ended it with him before, he had always been the one who said "It's over." But I beat him to it and he was going to make me pay.

"It's just a dick *thang*, you wouldn't understand."

"Well baby, here I am try me..." I challenged, but he simply repeated himself. It wasn't about our relationship at all but about Troy's bruised ego. There was nothing more to say. I left him to play with his 'dick *thang*' and made my way the three and a half blocks through the winter snow to my apartment, wondering about Troy's Jekyll and Hyde transformation from kind and considerate lover to spiteful ex. As far as I was concerned, Troy was history.

So here I am a year later, a new year and on my way to starting a new life, strapped into a deep, leather, first class seat, 30,000 feet up in the air, Otis Redding declaring just how strong his love is down my headphones as I lose myself in the latest Terry McMillan novel. Sitting a few

1

feet away in the next aisle, 'Mr Ebony Man', leans across and touches my arm.

"It's a good book," he says cheerfully.

I look up briefly, but long enough to take in his features fully. I had noticed that sparkling, confident smile, the shiny bronze skin, the thin moustache, rich hazel eyes and smoothed back relaxed hair, almost as soon as I stepped into the first class compartment. He isn't just good looking, but also elegantly dressed in a dark suit, clearly tailored to fit his broad physique with ease. An upwardly mobile black man — my one weakness! He has to be an executive on a business trip or maybe an athlete with very good taste in formal wear. Either way he's the only other black person in first class and I was hoping there would be an opportunity to break the ice. I'm as curious to find out more about him as he is eager to strike up a conversation. After all, he could be frontin'.

I smile politely and drop my gaze back to the book. The brother will have to work harder than that.

"Everything Terry McMillan writes is good," he adds, "I must have read that three times already."

"She's not *that* good," I reply.

"No really, Alice Walker's serious and deep and Maya Angelou's poetic and all that, but Terry just tells it like it is from the woman's point of view. I'm sure that if more brothers were to read her they would appreciate the special woman in their life even more."

I put my book down and look into his eyes suspiciously, waiting for the punch line. Is this the latest pick-up line for a better class of black partner, I wonder with an unconvinced raise of my eyebrow, but the man seems earnest. He introduces himself, Andre Brown. To be precise, Lieutenant Andre Brown — the youngest

2

homicide officer in the Chicago Police Department. A cop with the dress sense of Gianni Versace? I raise my eyebrow higher, even more suspiciously. As if in reply, he pulls out a Chicago Police Department badge.

"I always wanted to be a cop, ever since I was a kid," he states, almost apologetically.

"I'm impressed, the Department must be paying its officers well nowadays," I say, catching a glimpse of the diamond studded Cartier beneath his shirt cuff.

"Oh the Mack Daddy pays for everything," he replies with a wide smile.

"Mack Daddy," I answer innocently, "who he?"

"Have you never heard of Mack Daddy? Lieutenant Mack Dadier, in the Mack Daddy detective novels?"

I draw a blank. Andre obliges further.

"The Mack Daddy thrillers are what some people call trash fiction. I write them in my spare time."

Andre produces a paperback book from a briefcase under his seat and hands it to me. 'Mack Daddy In The Bronx', I read the title to myself. I check out the cover photograph of a handsome black man who could have passed for Andre's brother, holding up a police ID badge in one hand and a smoking gun in the other. The back cover notes explain: 'When three homeboys are mysteriously clubbed to death in the South Bronx, a new jack cop is needed to solve the crime. Enter Lieutenant Mack Dadier, a ruffneck cop with attitude and his own set of rules...'

"So you're Andrew Berry?" I ask, reading the author's sleeve notes.

"One and the same," Andre answered, grinning from ear to ear. "Check this out... it pays the rent and a bit more."

He tugs at the lapels of his jacket as if to illustrate the

point. I noticed he didn't have a ring on his wedding finger. Maybe he sees the glint in my eye, maybe he doesn't, but I am impressed and definitely interested. Andre was more than just a pretty face and a natty dresser. This brother has class.

"Hi," I said stretching out a hand invitingly, "I'm Dee Robinson, I'm in advertising... Say, I'd like to hear more about your writing; would you like to sit over here so we can talk without the stewardess walking down the aisle every few seconds."

I made it sound like a joke, but I was serious. Andre seemed nice, the kinda man I'd been looking for in the last twelve months. Maybe I could still find Mr Right in America after all.

Getting a man isn't the problem. I haven't met a man yet who would turn down the chance to spend the night together if they were offered. But high calibre men are in short supply. They've either been snapped up already or they're not into women...

"You gotta be kidding me!" Glenda exclaimed down the line from San Francisco when I told her that I was taking the job in London. "Okay, maybe you won't find Mr. Right in Chicago, but you've got the whole of America to go looking, chile. If Chicago won't do, then try New York, LA, D.C... Why not move to Atlanta? Dee baby, that city is live! I just read an article in Essence which said that Atlanta has got the highest number of eligible, upwardly mobile black men in America. Sis, what you can't find in the U.S. you won't find overseas, believe me. Remember, I'm the one who Uncle Sam sent to Germany for three years. I *know*."

It's funny, I was always the one giving my younger sister advice — how to get through high school with as

4

little pain as possible, who to date, what to wear and how to survive and stay alive. When Glenda went into the army she was still the feisty teenager from Baton Rouge who together with two of her homegirls were known in our neighbourhood as 'triple trouble'. She came out of the Forces five years later as a card carrying all-American model citizen, married to Harvey — a six foot five marine and veteran of Operation Desert Storm. He's now a decorated sergeant and Glenda's a housewife bringing up twin three year old boys on an army salary, yet she feels obliged to help me find a man "just like Harvey." It's great having a kid sister who's your best friend, but when it comes to dating I don't need nobody else, I can do bad all by myself.

"I don't even know if there are any decent black men in London," Glenda continued down the long distance line. I told her there were. I had been over there the previous month to check things out.

"I met some pretty cool guys," I assured her. "And you know how the English are, right? They always sound so polite and educated... I just love that accent."

"Is that some kind of an admission?" Glenda teased. "Are you trying to tell me that you met someone 'in particular' over there?"

"No," I echoed, mimicking her, "nobody 'in particular', sis... I just have a good vibe about London. I had a great time over there and I think the change is going to be good for me — the experience, the places to see, new people to meet..."

"Well honey, I love my African-American man too much to go fishing in a smaller pond."

Now when I think about it, maybe Glenda was right. Maybe I hadn't given the U.S. male a fair chance. But I had lost patience with the brothers. I couldn't keep going around in circles, dating men who couldn't deal with an independent black woman who earns more money than they do. I worked hard to get to where I am, I should be able to enjoy my money in any way I please, but every man I've met seems to find that a problem, especially since I became creative director at Frazier Clarke Advertising. Being a success is great, but I want to share it with someone. That doesn't mean I'm going to hang around for that person to come. Where I'm at in my life right now, finding a partner is important, but not everything.

Troy was really happy for me when I got the job. We had been seeing each other on and off for a few weeks at the time. He worked as press secretary in the City Hall office of Chicago's black mayor Richard Wilkins. I was working as a copywriter for the mayor's springtime re-election campaign. The first time the tall, athletic Denzel Washington lookalike suggested that we discuss the media campaign over lunch. It turned out to be the first of many casual rendezvous before we *formally* decided that we were dating at a victory reception after the elections where Oprah and Steadman were among the invited guests. Dressed in a tux, Troy looked elegant and teased me all evening that if we were married he'd make sure I wore the same Yves St Laurent dress for dinner every evening. As we danced to the live Dixie jazz band, he gently pulled me close to him and kissed me lightly on the lips. It wasn't the first time we had kissed, but this time it felt more intimate. I knew what was going down, we both did. And Troy knew that I knew. I wanted it also, I wanted it bad. We held hands discreetly throughout the evening, but by the end of it Troy was holding me tightly enough to be noticed. 'It won't be long now', I figured, maybe an hour, maybe sooner, that Troy would be able to slip away from the reception unnoticed, we would be undressing each other slowly either in my apartment or his, I didn't mind which. I thought about his toned, strong body gripping me tightly, the taste of his sweat and the warmth of his breath on the nape of my neck. Every part of me seemed to tingle in anticipation, I could barely wait.

"No really Dee, writing a novel ain't that difficult," Andre insisted.

We had only been talking ten minutes but already we were chatting away like old friends. Andre had so much to say and had a way of talking that made what he was saying sound like the most interesting thing.

We shared the joke when we discovered that we had both had our first class tickets paid for by our respective employers. Andre was on his way to Paris, as he had been invited to lecture to a criminology class at the University there.

"I speak French," he said defensively, reading my thoughts. *"Est-ce que vous parlez francais aussi?"*

A linguist as well? Could he really be this perfect?

"But didn't you have to go on a writing course to learn how to write novels?"

"Sure I could have, but I didn't. Look, you wanna know how I started writing... it was because of my niece Jennifer,my sister's daughter. She's only ten years old but she loves reading detective novels. I don't know why, she's just one of those bright kids who outgrew all the books for her age group too fast. So every time I go over to babysit, I like to buy her a really good paperback thriller. But I also want her to have a balanced education because most of the learning she gets in school is culturally biased, that's when I discovered that there are hardly any black detective novel writers. Did you know that?"

I shook my head. It hadn't even occured to me. Andre continued...

"She's read all the Chester Himes books and she loved that stuff, you know, because she could relate to it. And she's read all of Walter Moseley's novels and she even figured out the endings before she came to them; remember this is one bright kid. So I've run out of ideas and I'm due to babysit the next week. Fortunately I had a few days off and one day I just decided to sit down in front of my computer and write my own detective novel with an ending she couldn't figure out."

"And did you succeed?" I asked, totally engaged in the conversation. Despite my secret fear of flying, I barely noticed the turbulence which tossed the jumbo about like a paper plane.

"Boy did I succeed," Andre laughed. "She had to keep reading until the last page to solve the crime..."

A stewardess announced over the cabin intercom that we had passed the turbulence and that the captain had now switched off the 'fasten safety belt' sign. I caught myself searching a little too deeply into Andre's eyes. He noticed also and smiled, a warm, embracing smile. All the time I was wondering if life could really be so cruel as to torment me like this. Here I was flying to London a single woman with the 'man I've been looking for' sitting right next to me on his way to Paris via New York. Andre had good looks, style, manners, intelligence, ambition, good prospects *and* he wrote novels! My old sorority girlfriends from Michigan State would die if I told them about this. A writer was the kind of man we all fantasised about settling down and starting a family with.

"You must have been a pretty bright child too," I

offered. "To be able to just pick up and start writing, you've got to be smart, right? Were you always interested in writing as a kid?"

"That's just it, I wasn't," Andre said.

Andre did his best to assure me that he was just a regular guy. He didn't think he was doing anything special when he investigated a homicide, neither did he think he was doing anything exceptional when he wrote any of the Mack Daddy thrillers. If he could pick up a pen and start writing a novel, anybody could, he insisted. His niece enjoyed the first Mack Daddy story so much that she gave it to her mother to read. She also enjoyed it and sent it to a literary agent. The next thing he knew, a black publishing company called Rex Publishing who had just set up an office in New York had offered a deal on it.

"Did you say you're flying off to London?" Andre asked. "You should check out those guys, you know, because they're from over that side. They're just a couple of regular guys with a jammin' little company putting out books for the black community. They're always saying they want more novels from women, so when you're in London, if you come up with an idea call them up."

I laughed modestly.

"The most writing I've done is some copywriting for advertisements. I couldn't write a novel."

"Why not?" Andre retorted. "What's the difference? You've got stories to tell haven't you?"

"Definitely... lots of stories. But writing's not my thing. I prefer to read Terry McMillan than write myself."

"Well my view," Andre countered, "is that we need more black stories for the kids coming up to read. We've got no time to waste."

Troy and I had had a good thing going. We were both young, successful and ambitious. We were both perfectionists and shared a love for modern jazz, Italian cooking and African art. And we were both great conversationalists so we rarely shared a dull moment together. It *seemed* like our relationship wasn't affected by the usual pitfalls of money worries and infidelity. For the first six months especially, I was thanking the Lord for answering my prayers and sending me the most eligible man in Chicago. He had ambition, a life plan. He had a master's degree in law from Howard University but he had his sights on higher things than a career in the legal profession. His job in charge of Mayor Wilkins' PR was a stepping stone to what he really wanted to do — become a politician himself eventually. A committed Democrat, Troy wanted to 'increase the peace' in Chicago's South Side by lobbying big business to pay for improved education and better job opportunities for the community they were earning so much from. He was only a couple of years older than me and was already being spoken about in Illinois' black political circles as one of the freshest stars on the horizon. And I wasn't doing too badly either with my career in corporate advertising. We were the 'perfect couple' at all the social gatherings we attended and many of my girlfriends envied me for having him.

But then I got promoted to creative director after the success of my Color Creatives caption: 'Black By Popular Demand'. Suddenly I had all this power at one of the top advertising agencies in the mid-west and a high roller salary to go with it. In fact I ended up earning much more than Troy. He kept telling me how proud he was to know that his woman was "kickin' it and maxin' " in the advertising industry. Slowly, things started changing in our relationship; suddenly it was me that was getting

10

invited to different functions and Troy was accompanying me as *my* partner. He didn't like that and I soon had to get used to attending the various industry parties on my own. It didn't take long before the media started getting interested in the 'dynamic young creative director' from Frazier Clarke. In an industry with very few black men or women in meaningful positions, I made an immediate impact.

Things really began to change between me and Troy after the lifestyle article that Essence magazine did on me. Somehow it seemed to bug Troy that I had described him in the interview as my partner.

"How could you say that! How could you say that!" he raged after reading the piece.

"Well, it's true isn't it?" I asked incredulously. "That's exactly what you are so I didn't see any point in denying it. I can't understand why you're so upset."

We were lying in bed in my apartment doing the Chicago Sun crossword together when Troy picked up that month's issue of Essence. Any desire to get more intimate disappeared as he read the article.

"I have my career to think about as well, you know Dee," he replied angrily. "I am Troy Adams, not Mr Dee Robinson. I don't intend to be 'the man behind the successful woman', because I happen to be pursuing my own political ambitions. Don't you think you owed me the courtesy of asking me first before you started discussing my private life in a national magazine?"

"Oh get real, Troy," I reasoned, "it was only an interview, I think you're over-reacting to this. If you don't want me to mention your name again, I won't. Anything you say, I just don't have time to argue about this."

It didn't end there. The article left a sour taste in Troy's mouth for a long time afterwards. Suddenly he began to

11

complain that I was spending too much time at work and too little time in the relationship.

"Baby I'm really happy for the way your career is taking off, but where does that leave me? Where does that leave us? Do you expect me to hang around and wait for you to reach the top of the career ladder or what, because it doesn't seem like you've got much time to devote to making things work between us."

I could hardly believe my ears. Troy, who was single-minded about becoming the first black president of the United States and who had looked on our relationship almost as a hobby to devote time to whenever he had a minute, was now upset that I was making use of all the opportunities open to me in my career also.

"What the hell are you saying Troy, are you saying that this relationship isn't working, is that what you're saying?"

I was angry, fuming and left Troy in no doubt that I wasn't going to take this crap. He backpeddled a bit. No, he wasn't saying that exactly... It was just that he felt that I had changed with my new job and new responsibilities and new salary and he wasn't sure if he liked the way I had changed.

Ever the politician, even in his personal affairs, Troy was making it sound like he was saying all this for my sake. But I read between the lines and new that the problem was something more fundamental. The notion of power had changed in our relationship. All that had happened was that I had been promoted at work, something that happens to people every day. But the reality of that situation was that I had ended up earning much more money than my partner and Troy — like so many millions of other men — had not been brought up to be able to deal with that. Nobody had ever told him

12

that life could be like that. He didn't want to admit that he was on the macho 'black man as a breadwinner' tip, but that's really where he was coming from. You could tell from the stream of horse manure that poured out of his mouth as he searched for a way to redeem himself.

"Dee baby, I want you to be successful and all that, but you gotta see things from my point of view. You're my squeeze; I thought we had something strong together, that maybe someday you would walk down that aisle and find me waiting at the alter in front of the preacher. That's what I want to happen. I want us to settle down and have a home and raise some kids together. But I can't see how that's possible anymore. Since you got promoted you've had your mind on work and I can't see when you'll be able to find the time to settle down now that you're a high-flying advertising executive."

All this came as a shot out of the blue to me, as my expression revealed. Since when did Troy start thinking about marriage and kids, and why was he only saying this to me now? Once again he was making it sound like he was only trying to advise me. But I wasn't buying it.

"So how come the job I'm doing suddenly means I can't settle down when I want to?" I asked.

Troy searched around for an answer and avoided my gaze when he replied.

"Baby, I want to marry someone who's got time to spend thinking about me and taking care of me, someone who's got time to raise my kids, not someone whose job comes before her family. You know how it is Dee, a woman earning more than her partner is a recipe for tension and disaster."

Poor Troy, poor helpless modern man. It wasn't about kids and a family at all, but about economics, pure and simple. Instead of losing my cool, I took pity on him. For a man with so much education he had a lot to learn about sisters like me.

"Well that's just too bad," I said assertively, "black men better get used to that because their women are leaving them behind, earning double, three and four times more than they are and we're not taking any shit with it either."

"Well, let me see, you might have seen my magazine adverts for Karl Kani jeans, the ones with Naomi Campbell. I like working on advertisements like that, but you know, advertising is culturally biased also," I said.

The stewardess came over and filled up our champagne glasses again. I glanced at my watch. We would be landing in New York in ten minutes, but I wished the flight was longer, much longer. It seemed silly to be so interested in someone I had only known for such a short time, but I couldn't help it. As well as everything else, I was sure that Andre was the most charismatic man I had ever met! In the back of my mind I was telling myself that I didn't want to say goodbye to this man when we got to New York. I would exchange addresses with him before we went our separate ways and if he didn't have the chance to visit me in London, a dinner date with Andre would be top of my agenda whenever I returned to Chicago.

"In the old days none of the big corporations wanted black people in their advertisements. It was only when the black consumer started voting with their feet and taking their business and money elsewhere, that all these hamburger chains and soda companies suddenly realised how important the black dollar was to their business. But even now you would be surprised how many companies tell us that they only want us to use black models with as little African features as possible."

14

"Are you kidding?" Andre asked amazed.

"Sure. You must have heard the three cardinal rules of advertising: 'If you're white, that's alright, if you're brown stick around, but if you're black...'"

" 'Stay back'!" Andre completed the rhyme.

"Exactly."

"Do you enjoy working in an industry like that?"

"I have a great time, because advertisers with backward views usually know to stay well away from me. For as long as I can remember I had always wanted to be in advertising and now that they've put me in a position of power and I'm going to use it and enjoy it. It's like you said about writing novels, right now we need more black achievers in advertising, because the image that comes across to the kids isn't always positive."

At that precise moment I would rather not have been talking about work; there was so much more I would rather have been talking to Andre about — most of it pretty intimate stuff as well, but I had to leave all that to my imagination for the sake of decorum. We hardly knew each other and I couldn't afford to be seen as an 'easy' woman.

A heavy snowstorm was falling as we descended on the JFK runway. It looked beautiful, with thick white flakes blotting out the early evening winter sky. I shifted my seat into the upright position and turned to Andre who was smiling at me inquisitively.

"Snow always makes New York look so clean," I said, as the plane eased itself down gently closer and closer to the terminal lights shining dimly below.

"Me too, I love it when it snows," Andre said, "...except when I'm flying."

With a violent shudder, the plane landed on the runway and seemed to skid uneasily for the longest time until the pilot managed to slow it down.

"You see what I mean?" Andre said as the aircraft ambled along to its allotted gate. "I like to think of myself as a real man, but when it comes to flying and snow I'm as nervous as a child."

"Well at least we've landed safely."

"It ain't over until the fat lady sings..." Andre warned.

It wasn't until we were inside the terminal that I understood what he meant by that. The snow was causing chaos on the runway. Ours was the last plane to land that day. The forecast was of more snow and there would be no more flights landing at or taking off from JFK until the morning at the earliest. The entire airport seemed to be in turmoil, with the ticketing desks besieged by irate travellers demanding more than a feeble excuse about the effects of weather. I wasn't about to pitch my lot in with everybody else so I began considering my options instead. I *could* call my cousin Ira all the way up in Harlem and stay there the night. It was a long way to travel and then have to come back out to the airport the next day. No, I decided, it would be better to stay at a hotel overnight and get on the first flight the next day. Fortunately Andre was still with me, unable to fly to Paris either. It was at this point that he revealed one of the advantages of having a police badge. Waving it ahead of him, he cut a clear path through the crowd of people and guided me along until we got to the ticketing desk at the end.

"Hi, Lieutenant Andre Brown of the Chicago Police Department," he said authoritatively to the woman behind the desk.

She examined the ID for a minute, obviously impressed that the handsome, young black man in front of her was a high-ranking police officer.

16

"How can I help you, Lieutenant?" she asked.

"My assistant and I," Andre began, indicating in my direction, "are on our way to an important investigation in Europe — the outcome of which relies on us arriving fresh. Now I know that you can't do anything about getting us there tonight, but I insist that you find us decent hotel rooms nearby as a matter of courtesy. We both have first class tickets and that's the least you can do."

The woman behind the desk looked incredulous, but she could see that Andre was serious. The crowd behind him had hushed and watched bemused as the woman picked up the phone on her desk and dialled to her superiors. After a moment she put down the phone and smiled politely at Andre.

"Lieutenant, the airline would like to offer you and your assistant complimentary rooms at the Larriot Hotel for tonight," she said handing him a couple of vouchers. "If you just walk through the exit doors behind you, you'll find the courtesy limousine to take you to the hotel."

Andre turned to me and smiled. I smiled back, impressed. Andre certainly knew how to take care of himself. The crowd around stood stunned, but suddenly, as we made our way out of the exit door, everyone else rushed the woman behind the desk demanding rooms too.

Things never improved with Troy. Looking back on those last few months together, I can't understand why we didn't just end it. I guess that Troy still had most of the wonderful qualities I had admired in him in the beginning. He was still intelligent, he still had the potential to be an important black political figure in

17

America and he could still be charming and witty when he wasn't competing with me. For his part, I reckon he had no reason to end the relationship. I had attended so many social functions with him where people were just as interested in meeting me as they were in Troy. I had become a political asset. Unfortunately, Troy was consumed by the need to assert himself in our relationship. He was still talking garbage. My favourite one was, "Women who have more money than their partners are more likely to be unfaithful!"

I humoured him, hoping he would come to terms with things. Instead, he became increasingly distant and moody and just wasn't interested in in the same things as me anymore. The little time we spent together became fraught with tension.

It all reached a head that Thanksgiving a year ago when we were having dinner together for the first time in weeks at Luigi's, one of the top restaurants in downtown Chicago. I had hoped that we could make each other laugh and happy again, as we used to, without the baggage of our individual careers dragging us down.

Suddenly in the middle of the main course, as the waiter filled our wine glasses, Troy dropped his bombshell:

"Kids..."

"What?!"

"Haven't you ever felt that way Dee? Like despite everything you've done in life, in your job and with all your possessions there's still something missing... I just feel that I want to start a family and start one now... with you."

Uh-huh! So now he wants kids and he wants them now. Well go ahead, Troy, I ain't stoppin' you. You get pregnant, and you give up your job to look after your child.

18

"When you've been in a relationship a while, you have to either get married and have kids or end it," Troy implored, "otherwise what else is there?"

Married! Kids! It had still not sunk in. This wasn't how I had expected a proposal to be and this wasn't the time I would have wanted to get a proposal either. I didn't even have to think about it, I knew my answer already. I loved the freedom of the lifestyle I enjoyed riding the shooting star of my career and I didn't want it changed and I certainly didn't want a kid coming in the middle of it! Like any thirty-year-old woman I had felt that biological clock ticking away once or twice and knew that I wanted a baby eventually. But at that moment there were enough hassles in my life without bringing in new ones. I also knew that despite his words, the idea of a child scared the hell out of Troy. It always had. It was he who had made it clear when we first started dating that he wanted things to be uncomplicated and that one of the things that had attracted him to me in the first place was that I seemed to be different from all the other women he had dated who had wanted kids at the end of the relationship. So why the big change? Troy denied that it was about trying to make sure that I wouldn't earn more money than him and hence couldn't be 'unfaithful'.

Instead he became defensive and uncharacteristically coarse when I said I was more interested in my career than becoming a housewife.

"You'd better think about it a bit longer," Troy said. It sounded like a threat. "Because yeah, this is something that I would end the relationship over."

I couldn't believe that he could be so arrogant. I sat silently for a moment before I responded.

"There's no need for you to end the relationship Troy, it's over. Nobody talks to me like that. You understand

19

Troy? I'd be crazy if I married you and had kids with you. You want a wife that is inferior to you, someone you can push around. Honey, I ain't tha' one."

Troy wasn't expecting what he heard. He took a deep breath and I could almost see the anger rise up from the pit of his stomach and rush up to his head.

"Bitch!" he hissed. "You're so high and mighty with your big job and your big salary, but all you are to me now is a bitch anyway."

I was taken aback and looked around embarrassed, but the other diners were consumed in their own conversations. As always, Troy was careful to maintain a discreet tone of voice.

"You think a bitch like you could really get a man like me? Bitch. You weren't even that good in the sack, that's why I had to go balling a different babe every week. You didn't know that did you? Well now you do. Get real bitch, it was just a dick *thang*."

I had heard enough. Before he had a chance to react, I had grabbed the carafe of red wine on the dining table and turned it upside down on his head, emptying its contents. I paused for only a beat to admire my work before turning and marching out through the restaurant, watched by the other stunned diners. I tried to resist crying as I hurriedly made my way home, but it was easier said than done. Fresh tears melted a trail back to my apartment that Thanksgiving.

When I realised that I would have more time with Andre, I said quietly to myself, "Thank you Lord." I had forgotten about the delay in my journey, there would be lots of flights the next day. I reasoned, on the way to the hotel in the limousine, that I probably wouldn't decline an invitation to spend the night with Andre if one arose.

From the glint in his eye when the man at the hotel check-in asked if we were together and would like to share a suite, I guessed that Andre was thinking along the same lines as me. He looked across to me and winked, before informing the man that we were "just good friends."

'Good friends!' GOOD FRIENDS!? That's the last thing I want to hear, but the night is still young and I haven't made myself totally irresistible yet...

We agreed to meet down in the hotel bar in two hours, which would give us time to freshen up and take a little nap. Once in my room, I fell on the bed exhausted and for a moment just lay on my back, looking up at the ceiling — wondering whether going to London was really the right decision or whether, new job aside, what I was looking for was right here in the United States after all.

After ending things with Troy, I hadn't found another permanent relationship, but had been 'between relationships' for almost a year. As ever there seemed to be a limitless supply of men available, especially when word got around that I was on the single's market again. My network of friends and family made sure that every eligible man they came across got my number. But finding the right man... that was a different matter. For one reason or another each romantic encounter fizzled out after one or two dates.

The main problem seemed to be that I was making more money than most of the men I dated. Like Trevor, a 30-year-old TV producer who thought his penis made up for the difference in our incomes. He didn't need to deal with the problems in our relationship because his manhood wasn't just power to him, but was also worth at least $100,000 more than I was earning. A man who takes his penis that seriously does nothing for me. I didn't want to waste time with someone I really wasn't into, while the interesting men were slipping away. Trevor lasted a month.

My experience with him taught me to be increasingly discreet on the subject of money with the men I dated. Even with Lance — a 33-year-old corporate lawyer earning a six-figure salary, who liked to play as hard as he worked and seemed in every respect to be my intellectual and social equal. I soon realised that his designer clothes and expensive cars were mere status symbols but in his mind they were quality contributions to our relationship. He didn't feel that he needed to work on feelings and emotions. He didn't like to show his feelings and couldn't deal with anyone else's feelings, even his woman's. Then he started to be less giving of himself. I knew what I was worth on the singles market and felt I deserved more than all the expensive presents Lance had bought me. But asking him what was on his mind was all too much pressure for him and one night he called and said he wanted to end the relationship.

Things went kinda quiet for me in Chicago after Lance and I broke up. I didn't think it would leave me feeling empty inside but I had invested too much emotion in those three months together to simply shrug my shoulders...

I went through a few more one night specials, before deciding that I simply didn't have the time for them and that I had too much to do job-wise, for these short bursts of sexual exploration.

Chicago began to feel stale and I began considering moving on. I called around to some of my girlfriends, sorority sisters who I had kept in touch with since college, after we had each gone our different ways to pursue our dreams. Larianne who was teaching in DC, warned me down the long distance line that she hadn't met a man worth talking about in six months. "The black man is in short supply in this city baby, you better keep your little ass in Chicago, girlfriend." LaToya, who had moved down South after college to marry her millionaire record producer twice her age and then divorced him a year later and become extremely rich in the process, urged me to come down and check Atlanta out, "Our cup runneth over with black men," she joked down the line, "but the competition is stiff for the successful, upwardly mobile, single black male, honey. They're snapped up as soon as they come on the market."

The more I phoned around the more I was convinced of taking the advertising job in London. There were too many attractive, successful, ambitious and upwardly mobile black women in America, sitting around with passion in their hearts, waiting in vain for the right guy. I wasn't about to let myself go to waste because of a man or by the lack of a man. London sounded like a cool city with no guns and little violence, where people were polite to each other and there was much more history and culture than Chicago. And the job at Splash was too good a career move to turn down.

"Why is it that men are prepared to risk everything they've got in a relationship — love, their woman, even their children — for one careless night with another woman? Why is that?"

Andre raised up his hands innocently.

"Hey, hold on, you have all kinds of men out there. Don't put us all in the same bag."

We had found a table in a dimly-lit section of the piano bar, from where we could hear the delicate vocal tones of the happy-faced brother on the keyboards, singing a

23

seventies selection of soulful ballads. *Me & Mrs Jones* wafted across the room.

"But it's true, men cannot control their sexual urges," I continued, taking a sip from the champagne that the hotel had provided on the house once they had discovered that Andre was a high ranking police officer from Chicago on an international mission.

"How about the women?" Andre asked.

"What...?"

"I mean, I know a lot of women who also can't control their sexual urges."

Andre was muscular but elegant even when he wore black slacks and a cashmere sweater. I had changed into a wool jumper long enough to wear as a dress and knee-length black boots which never failed to attract attention.

"But they don't tend to risk everything that is dear to them just for sex. There are two many talented attractive sisters sitting around getting dissed by men who can't see further than gratifying their sexual desires."

Andre smiled again. He was still charming, even though some of his views were typical male stuff — nothing that I couldn't re-programme with a little time!

"You know what, you can spend your life trying to find a man who would never be unfaithful, but you'll miss a lot of good possibilities. If fidelity is the most important thing to you then go for it, but if not, you might end up cutting your nose to spite your face."

"It's easier for a man to say that. Because in a man's world he gets his props if he has more than one woman. But women don't get praise for that sort of thing. Would you introduce a woman that had more than one man to your mother?"

"The fact remains," Andre went on, "that underneath all our differences in approach, men and women want the same thing at the end of the day. You want to be loved, I want to be loved. You want to be cared for, so do I and we both want to be respected and appreciated."

"Ain't that the truth," I punctuated, distantly.

Me & Mrs Jones came to an end and the pianist followed almost immediately with The Chi-Lites' *Have You Seen Her?* Andre paused for a second and had to admit that his mother wouldn't like it.

Tonight was special, almost magical. I felt so good about being with Andre as champagne mixed with talk and laughs into the early hours of the morning. By the time the pianist had sung the final verse of *When I Fall In Love*, doing a perfect impersonation of Nat King Cole, we were the only couple left in the piano bar, with chairs piled on tables all around us. Light-headed from the champagne we made our way out of the bar arm in arm and through the foyer where we waited for the elevator. Andre looked good enough to eat. As the elevator doors closed behind us, a thought crossed my mind. Andre must have been thinking the same thing:

"It's been such a romantic evening..." he began unsteadily as the elevator raced up the floors. "I wish somehow that it could continue..."

He paused and stared hard at me.

"You know what I mean?"

Yes, I know exactly what you mean. There's magic in the air and champagne always makes you want the evening to go on forever.

"I would want nothing more than for this evening to continue, but..."

Oh no, I've heard this before.

"...I'm unavailable right now. I'm engaged and in love with my fiancee."

I should have known. Men like Andre aren't just walking

25

around without a woman waiting at home.

"So what's she like?" I asked, trying to contain my envy.

"Oh Shawna? She's fun, you know, we have a good time together."

Andre had a look of warmth in his eyes as he spoke.

Typical; well hopefully you're about to tell me that the two of you fight all the time, and she snores!

I decided not to ask any more questions about his fiancee, I had heard enough. His life in Chicago was a thousands miles away and at that moment I preferred that it remained there.

"I'm a faithful kinda guy... even when I know my woman won't find out..."

Suddenly I sobered up. What was I doing? My time spent with Andre had been so perfect that I wanted to spend my last few hours in the United States with him. Lying in bed beside him, with his powerful arms around me and my head on his chest, listening to his heart beat. I was even prepared to forget that he was another woman's man.

"Well I'll be sad to see you go," I said to Mr Oh-so-fine-but-taken-by-another-woman, trying to hide my disappointment. "I'm leaving early tomorrow morning." I handed him a company business card from my handbag. "If you're ever in London, look me up."

"Hey, you know what Dee, I've had such a great time tonight. When you get back to Chicago call me at the precinct and we'll do dinner. When I get back, I'll make sure that I send you the complete Mack Daddy series of books to the address on this card, okay?"

We embraced each other as if we were old friends, warmly and tightly. Then I slipped my key card into the lock.

26

"Have a safe journey," he said as he made his way to his room.

"Hey!" I called after him teasingly.

He spun around, waiting.

"Oh... nothing."

The next day I flew to London with a hangover. I thought that I had found the right man six months too late.

SHAME AND PRIDE

Carol sighed nervously and looked at her watch again.

"If you just take a seat Ms Ballantine, Miss Ridgley will be with you in a moment," the receptionist said with a polite smile.

Carol sat down, placing her shoulder bag down carefully. She hardly noticed the two tense-looking white youths dressed as formally as was expected for any job interview, who were eyeing her cautiously, 'sizing up' the competition. Carol had her mind on other things. She had used her maiden name so as not to arouse suspicion.

If she had considered them for a moment, she would have had every confidence that she was at least as well dressed as they were, having chosen to wear her navy business suit and a simple white blouse with a blue and white polka dot scarf around the collar and sensible black shoes. Today, it didn't bother her that she no longer wore the suit well, that the weight she had put on over the Christmas period had turned it into a loosely tightened girdle.

At the age of 34 and after nearly eight years of marriage, Carol Edwards was suddenly faced with being a single woman again. Neville, her husband, had decided to drop the news that he was leaving her, on Christmas Eve, just as she was preparing what *was* to have been a family Christmas. His parents had been invited and also his brother who was coming with his own wife and two kids. Her mother was also going to be there. She had bought all the presents, the food and all the little things that they would need with seven extra people to entertain. She had planned to cook a special Christmas jollof rice with spicy turkey cutlets. The whole family knew that Carol's cooking skills were unparalleled and with the children's love of her desserts in mind, she intended to make a strawberrry tea cake with ice cream for them. Despite the sad significance of Christmas Day for her and her husband, Carol had been determined to make sure that they would be as happy as possible. As always, Neville had left all the finer details to her. He was too busy with work right up to Christmas Day, to have time to help her with the Christmas tree and decorations which she was hanging up even as he broke the news to her.

"I've got another woman and I'm leaving you today," he said. "You can have the house, but that's it. Everything will probably turn out alright for you."

Standing on a stool, straightening up the star at the top of the tree, Carol thought she had misunderstood what he was saying. Lately Neville hadn't been able to make up his mind one way or another about their life together. He would say contradictory things like: "I love you, but I'm not *in love* with you," "you're the woman in my life, but I don't love you," "you're my sister, my friend and my lover, but not my woman," and "we are *too* close to each other, we've become *too* close, *too* intimate."

She turned to face him. He simply stared at her seriously, waiting for a response. Then it hit her, the look on his face... she had heard clearly alright. As the penny dropped, Carol's legs gave way.

The weekends Neville had spent playing fly-half for his company rugby team, came in useful. He dived across the room and only just caught his wife as she was falling off the stool.

29

"Oh shit!" he exclaimed, as he pulled her over to the sofa.

A moment later, Carol opened her eyes, staring up at Neville. The irritated expression on her husband's face made something snap inside her and unable to control herself, she lifted her head up and spat in his face. Before he was able to react she was on top of him, raining down blows about his ears and face as hard as her strength would allow. Neville, though much stronger, was caught by surprise and had little chance of protecting himself against those first painful blows.

"You, bastard! Bastard!!" Carol screamed again and again as she continued to strike out at all of Neville's sensitive areas. When he managed to grab hold of her arms, it was only for a moment. Before he knew it, his wife had turned to face him again as she directed a well-aimed knee in his groin. Then she was on his chest and throwing her fists in his face again. "You bastard! You bastard! Bastard! Bastard!" she repeated with every punch. With tears streaming down her face, clouding her vision, she didn't see Neville lift his elbow up and shove it with all his force into her face. The blow lifted Carol cleanly off of him.

Neville lifted himself up shakily, his teeth red with blood.

"You stupid cow!" he cried out. "What did you make me do that for?"

He didn't even wait for an answer but proceeded to go up to the bedroom to pack together a few clothes. From there it was into the bathroom for his electric toothbrush and shaver. He paused in front of the mirror to examine the damage Carol had done to him. His usually immaculate appearance was the worse for the beating he had taken. Bruises had knocked the shine off his face and his Bruce Oldfield pinstripe two-piece suit was not only bloodied but its pockets hung by the lining also. He spat out a mouthful of bloody saliva and examined his teeth once more in the mirror. They were still red. He kissed his teeth then went next door into his study, where he packed his papers and a few books. He jumped down the stairs, taking them three at a time, with his belongings all stuffed into the rucksack over his shoulder. He didn't want to waste time in the house. Not when his wife was acting like a maniac.

"You've got yourself to blame," he said without pity, pausing to stand over his shaken wife who was still lying on the carpet surrounded by tinsel and other decorations from the Christmas tree. "You're to blame for the death of my son... Think about it, if Junior was alive I'd be at home with the kid, being a father. Remember that when you're cursing me tonight. Take a look at yourself, you've become a fat cow. Do you really think any man would want you now? You've got to be kidding."

Neville saw his wife searching frantically for a missile. He lightfooted out of the door into the snowstorm outside, as a heavy ashtray sailed through the air behind him, slamming into the hurriedly closed front door with a crash.

"You're so full of shit!" she shouted angrily after him. She fell back on the carpet, exhausted, looking up at the ceiling, at the chandelier which she had had wired in the living room especially for Christmas. For some reason she began to think about all the arrangements for the next day. Should she call everybody up and cancel? Or should she go ahead with it and inform everyone when they arrived that Neville had left her? Compared to the breakdown of her marriage, the seasonal gathering seemed insignificant.

31

Neville's last words haunted her; how could he have been so cruel? However little he thought of her, she didn't deserve to hear that she was to blame for Junior's death, especially on the eve of the first anniversary of that tragic day. Neville was ignorant, but knew what impact his words would have. Still lying face up on the carpet, she burst out crying. Her arms and legs were heavy and cramped and her face had begun to swell and throwb with pain. In between her heart-wrenched sobs, she called out the name of the son she had carried for nine months, the son she had nurtured, cared for and watched over for five years, that part of her which was now buried deep in a cold grave.

For those who have to live with it, sickle cell is a dread illness. The doctors equate the pain suffered in a sickle cell crisis with that of a woman undergoing natural childbirth. Every sickler learns to live with this pain. Little Junior had bravely faced death before when a crisis had resulted in a heart attack. He finally succumbed to a sudden sickling in the brain, his young life ending on Christmas Day. Carol was devastated. For five years she had watched helplessly each time her son had cried with pain as sickling had attacked his chest and his knees with a vengeance. Hospitals had become a part of her life but her heart still pounded with fear every time she climbed into an ambulance to accompany him to casualty. The doctors had warned that every crisis was potentially fatal, directly if not indirectly, as it slowly wore down other organs. It was not something you could discuss with a five-year-old and Carol had frequently found herself agonising when Junior begged her to "make the pain go away."

She didn't know anything about sickle cell. Through leaflets she learned the disease was found amongst people from countries with the malaria mosquito, Africans especially. When 25 million Africans were kidnapped and shipped to far off corners of the world as slaves, sickle cell genes followed, replenishing themselves through the bloodstream, handed down from generation to generation as a malicious reminder of where they really come from whether black, brown, red, yellow, mellow or damn near white, and whether born in the Caribbean, in the States or wherever.

As far as Neville was concerned, nobody in his family had ever had sickle cell anaemia and despite the trait found in his bloodstream, he refused to accept that he was anything to do with his young son's illness. He blamed everything on his wife. After all, not only did she have the trait, but she also had a history of sickle cell in her family. This created a recurring tension in a marriage which had once had all the prospects of being the 'perfect relationship'.

From then on Neville became more and more irritable with everything his wife did. He saw faults in all of her actions and criticised her for being too timid one minute and too aggressive the next or for being too clever one minute and too stupid the next. On top of that, she was getting fat and her clothes weren't sitting on her properly, which annoyed him.

"Our sex life is shit," he complained one night after they had made love. "Is it?" she answered, hurt, but in agreement. Their sex life was shit, their love life was shit and everything about their relationship seemed to be shit these days.

They had met while at university. Neville had been a handsome economics student studying for an MBA when Carol was a first year law student. He had met her at the freshers' ball, just as she was regretting not having applied to a bigger city university. It wasn't that Durham University was a poor institution. On the contrary, it was one of the finest colleges in the country but in the few days she had been up there, she had come to realise that she was probably not going to see much black culture — that social, political and historical awareness that was as vital to her as the air that she breathed and the food that she ate. Durham was too dry as a town and the university desperately needed a Black Student's Alliance.

All her friends back home in Tottenham had said that university would change her totally, that when she came back she would not want to socialise with them. Frankie was clearly the most worried because he had the most to lose. He and Carol had been together since school and he soon claimed that she was not the girl he had fallen in love with anymore. Unlike him, she no longer put raving as high upon her list of priorities and she was too engrossed in "all this studying business." But Carol was adamant about becoming the first person in her family to go to university.

At the freshers' ball, Neville had asked for a dance as smoochy soul ballads replaced the diet of hi-energy blasting through the speakers. He was also from London and Carol was relieved that here was someone that she at least shared something in common with.

"You're not going to believe this," Neville began in a middle class accent, as they danced slowly and closely on the floor, "but my ex-girlfriend from last year is over by the bar with her new man."

Carol's eyes followed Neville's finger pointing to a tall, leggy blonde girl who was exchanging loving looks with a broad shouldered white guy.

"She's trying to make me jealous... The relationship is over and everything but she's playing games."

Carol simply carried on dancing, not knowing what all of this had to do with her. She was only dancing with the man, and really didn't feel like hearing about his ex.

"Would you mind if I kissed you?" Neville said suddenly.

"What?!" Carol couldn't believe what she had heard.

"It's just that I want her to get the message once and for all that it's over."

Carol looked at him closely, studying his eyes which were close up to hers. He had a cheek to ask her. Why didn't he just ask her straight for a kiss? Why did he have to involve her in his jealousy game?

"That's got to be the worst chat-up line I've ever heard," Carol answered suspiciously.

She declined the invitation. She had come up to university to get a degree and she didn't intend to be seen cavorting with someone she knew very little about in her first week.

After that first encounter, Neville had kept his distance from her for most of the rest of their time at university. He spent his time playing rugby and cricket and only bumped into Carol a few times in the library when they would always exchange a few pleasantries. He would ask how she was doing in her course work, but nothing more and she would enquire about the college's sporting successes just to be friendly.

Carol didn't see him again after that first year. He finished his degree and went back to London. One of his friends at college had mentioned that he had got a job in the city. Carol got on with her studying for the next two years. There were few distractions for a young black woman up in Durham, so she kept herself very much to herself, spending a lot of time in the college library, searching out 'additional reading' and consuming as much information as she could. Every now and then when she could afford it she travelled down to London to visit family and friends and to salvage what she could of her increasingly alienated relationship with Frankie, who after all was her first proper boyfriend.

Graduation was the highlight of her three years at Durham. Despite being separated, her parents forgot their differences and came up together for the occasion. Her father with tears in his eyes, cheered louder than any other parent when his daughter's name was called out during the ceremony. Nobody could have been more proud. All his years as a bus driver in England had been worth it for the moment of seeing his daughter walk confidently up to the university chancellor with a mortar board on her head and her long flowing black gown. Mrs Ballantine, Carol's mother, was quiet and smiling. Her heart crying the tears she refused to allow her eyes to shed. Her baby's finest hour was too precious to witness through misty eyes. She had worked hard to ensure that her children were not wanting. By day she typed schedule sheets at one of the government ministries and in the evening her job was as a mother: cooking and cleaning, doting and disciplining. Mrs Ballantine always knew that Carol would do well, but she had come out with flying colours. Very few of the other students called up to the stage had been awarded first class honours.

Five years later, Carol ran into Neville at a networking dinner for black professionals. The small basement wine bar off Regent Street was packed from wall-to-wall on this Wednesday evening with successful and up and coming careerists. It was Neville who introduced himself.

"You were at Durham weren't you?" he asked.

She didn't recognise him at first. He had shaved off the beard he used to have back at college and he was now dressed conservatively in a dark pinstripe suit and a little less formally with a pair of wide striped braces and a colourful tie.

"Don't tell me... I'll remember in a minute... It's on the tip of my tongue... Carol, you're Carol Ballantine."

"And you're Neville Edwards, I haven't forgotten you," Carol said recalling. "We danced together at the freshers' ball."

"Is that when we met?"

Neville had no recollection, and only faintly remembered the blonde-haired, blue-eyed leggy ex-girlfriend. He now worked for an American bank in the city, he explained, buying and selling currency. To him it was a job like any other, a means to an end — the end being to make enough money to retire by the age of 40 then spend the rest of his life doing all the things he really wanted to do.

"Weren't you reading law at college?"

Carol looked up, surprised that Neville could have remembered any details about her affairs at college. She nodded.

"But I now work as a researcher for Beverly Marshall," Carol said.

"The MP? That must be really interesting. But it can't be that well paid."

"I happen to like the job," she retorted, "I'm interested in pursuing a career in politics myself and this is the best way of getting a foot through the door and learning the ropes. Sure it doesn't pay well, but money isn't everything."

"No, but it's the only way black folk get respect in this country."

Carol had gone to network, but in the event she ended up talking with Neville for three hours. It was like they were old friends recalling all the characters they knew in common from their college days and how they had both wished that they had chosen to go to a university closer to home. He insisted on toasting her each time he held his wine glass, "to scholar Carol Ballantine," "to old acquaintances," "to new friendships." It was all done in good taste, and quite amusing, Carol felt. By the end of the evening, she had pushed the events of their first meeting at college far into the back of her mind and agreed to join him for dinner at his club in Soho the next week.

Neville proved to be the perfect gentleman holding car doors open for Carol and pulling her dinner chairs out before sitting down himself. After dinner he would help her on with her coat, all the time insisting that of course he knew she wasn't helpless but that he was being good-mannered out of respect and affection for her. It took several more dates though before Carol would agree to consider their relationship as anything but platonic. She enjoyed his companionship and his attention, he was everything she had wished Frankie to be — well-read, charming, eloquent and confident. Frankie had used every excuse not to better himself. After all, he had kept insisting, it was she who had changed while at university, as if his not having changed at all were some kind of virtue. But it wasn't — as her friends had predicted — university which changed her, it was education. She had spent three years at university doing what she most enjoyed doing, learning. University had afforded her the opportunity to contemplate the big picture at her leisure.

Carol had used the five years since breaking off with Frankie to take a break from men and relationships. She was more interested in travelling, her work and her girlfriends than she was in dating again. She and Frankie

38

had been together for so long that he still featured heavily in her thoughts. He even called several times over the first six months, hoping that she would reconsider, but it never got through to him that this woman did want him but only as her equal.

After five years, Carol had decided that she felt ready to be the focus of a man's attention again. In the months that followed, Neville proved that he knew how to treat a lady and that he was prepared to work hard to become her man. He would call her from work for no other reason than to say, "I love you," five times a day and he was always coming up with an interesting suggestion for spending an evening together: an evening at the theatre followed by a leisurely ferry cruise along the river afterwards. She finally consented to start seeing him officially after he sent 26 cards (one for each year of her age) on the morning of her birthday. Each card had a different message: 'You spice up my life — happy birthday!', 'I want you to get to know me better'. There was already a tulip with the message 'My lips long for yours', under the windscreen wiper of her car when she stepped out of the house. Carol smiled to herself when she read the card. She had to admit that she hadn't been romanced like this before. By her next birthday, she became Mrs Carol Edwards and moved into the cosy two-bedroom house in a fashionable part of Wimbledon, that Neville had bought with the help of a very favourable mortgage from his company.

Despite being married, they behaved as lovers for the first year, playing all the romantic games they had done before they started living together, like eating breakfast by candlelight and having dinner in bed. They were both overjoyed when Carol became pregnant. Neville was the proudest father-to-be in London and had already started making plans for his son, (he was sure it would be a boy) to be registered for Eton College at birth. In the evenings he returned home with a bottle of Dom Perignon to celebrate another day of his wife's pregnancy and when he had to go off to work in New York for a couple of weeks, he made sure that a fresh rose was delivered to his wife every morning with a different message on it.

Junior *seemed* to be a healthy child in every respect, except for his jaundiced eyes. The doctors soon discovered that this was sickle cell anaemia. Neville said that it was impossible. Didn't there have to be sicklers in both parents families before the child could inherit the disease? That wasn't the case the experts corrected. Both parents only had to have the sickle cell trait. Even after their blood tests, Neville was convinced that the doctors had made a mistake in his case, while his wife accepted the fact and that it would play a major part in Junior's life but she didn't aportion blame.

Nothing could have prepared either parent for the shock of seeing their son during a crisis. Their child was in and out of hospital continuously and despite the danger at his young age, he had undergone several blood transfusions.

Carol had no choice but to resign from her job as Beverly Marshall's researcher and stay at home to look after Junior full time. With Neville's recent promotion, he was earning more than enough money to support the family comfortably, so she didn't need to work for financial reasons.

Her relationship with her husband had changed. Carol noticed it, but he denied that it had anything to do with her. Neville said he was suffering the same pain in his head as his child was suffering in his joints and in his chest. Whatever her husband was going through, Carol knew that it was nothing like what Junior was suffering. The doctors had explained that sickle cell was like no other pain a human being suffers. She had joined a sickle cell organisation which had enabled her to talk to older sicklers. One veteran sufferer had described the pain in the chest as feeling like it was on fire and the pain in your joints as similar to someone stabbing you in the core of the bones in your body: "The pain is so intense," the woman had explained, "that if someone offered to chop your hand off to get rid of the pain, you would say 'yes'. The pain consumes your entire body. The painkillers don't help, at best they take the edge off the pain, but it is still there. Sometimes they don't have any impact at all."

It distressed Carol that her relationship with Neville had changed so much. They now rarely laughed and joked as they had previously done, they hardly went out anywhere together and they made love only occasionally and at the weekend. Neville simply didn't seem interested. He who had once said that he loved her curves was now saying that she was too fat. While she preoccupied herself with learning as much as she could about the illness that so regularly sent her child into hospital and every now and then making a feeble attempt at shedding the weight she had put on since childbirth with miracle diets, miracle milk shakes and powders and pills, Neville became an increasingly part-time husband.

Junior's illness seemed to abate every now and then, but it never went away and as he got older the pain of a crisis seemed to intensify. As a parent it was distressing to stand by helplessly, unable to do anything to ease the pain. Carol would have done anything to exchange places with her son. Neville would have also, but they couldn't.

After Junior's death, Neville became like a total

stranger in his marital home. Trying for any more kids was out of the question. Neville also refused to even consider Carol's suggestion that they should try to adopt. He wouldn't hear of it. If he couldn't have his own blood to continue after him, he wasn't interested. They weren't even sleeping with each other any more, because Neville began to take up the habit of sleeping in Junior's bedroom. In all of this he was entirely selfish and didn't seem to care how his wife felt. He suggested that she should go back to work even though he knew that it wouldn't be easy for her to get a job after five years at home. She couldn't even go back to her ex-boss Beverly Marshall, as she had now lost her place in parliament.

Carol hoped that someday her husband would come to terms with Junior's brief and painful life and carry on with their life as a couple. She tried everything to stimulate his interest in her again. They hadn't had sex for so long that she took matters in her own hand one evening . When Neville came home from work, Carol greeted him at the door wearing a big red ribbon and nothing else. Neville simply scowled when he saw her and closed the front door quickly behind him, in case the neighbours saw. Then he went up to his study room without giving her a second glance. He just wasn't interested and there was nothing she could do to change this. He was performing his marital duties by bringing home money every month and as far as he was concerned that should suffice. Carol spent her time meanwhile reading cook books and shopping for food. Neville behaved indifferently to her culinary creations, whether it was creamy mustard chicken and rice or his favourite old fashioned salmon pattied with broccoli sauce. Even though she indulged his penchant for cakes by baking everything from orange blueberry country muffins to blueberry coffee cakes, he resisted all her attempts to get to his heart through his stomach. Instead, Carol ended up with a craving for her own food.

Carol continued to give him enough rope, even when she discovered that he was having an affair. He had said that he was going on a trip to the bank's New York office. But he didn't even bother to cover his tracks. The two airline tickets fell out of his suit when she was emptying the pockets before taking it to the dry cleaners. The tickets weren't to New York at all, but to the Canary Islands.The second ticket was booked in the name of Ms J. Ridgley. When she called up Neville's office anonymously, she discovered that Miss Ridgley was Neville's secretary.

All this was at the beginning of December. Then Neville waited until Christmas Eve to announce that he was leaving her. After all they had been through, he felt no way about ruining her entire Christmas on the first anniversary of her son's death. Unable to face the family, Carol phoned around to everybody and cancelled the Christmas arrangements at the last minute. She had no desire to prepare a feast for anybody. Instead, she spent Christmas Day alone, thinking about her marriage, eating mince pies, a fruit cake and drinking rum and praying for her son who was no longer alive. Her heart yearned for Junior so much, she burst into tears whenever she thought about the brief time they had had together.

"Miss Ballantine?" the blonde woman asked with a pleasant smile when she came out to reception.

Carol looked up. She knew immediately that she had got the right woman.

"I'm Carol Edwards," she announced stiffly, "you've been sleeping with my husband."

The blonde woman's face dropped. She hadn't expected this. She looked about her nervously and at the other people in the reception area, hoping that Neville's wife wasn't about to create a scene.

"Perhaps we could talk about this some other time?" the woman said nervously.

"No, no other time. I just wanted to know if you make a habit of having affairs with married men and breaking up their homes, because if you do, people should know about it."

The woman didn't stand a chance. In one swift movement, Carol picked up her shoulder bag — throwing its contents over her rival's head. The black gloss paint went everywhere, on the carpet, the telephones, the windows and all over the secretary's long blonde hair and beige dress suit.

Carol didn't bother hanging around to admire her handiwork, but turned on her heels and made it hastily out of the office, wishing she had thrown the paint over Neville's head instead. But she felt so good about what she had just done that she skipped across London Bridge to catch her train back to Wimbledon.

Neville had already left a couple of angry messages on the answerphone by the time she got home, accusing her of being "neurotic". "You need your head examined!" he screamed down the line. "If you come near me or Jennifer again, I'll call the police."

Carol ignored the threats but went about the business of getting a locksmith in to change all the locks. She didn't know how she would do it, but she wanted to pay Neville back for way he had treated her.

DON'T HOLD YOUR BREATH

One thing I know for sure, I'm not going to be young forever. I've got to use what I've got to get to where I want to be, whilst I've still got it. Nobody's going to notice you in a small town like Bristol. You've got to go to where the action is — London.

When I finally decided to leave Wayne, it was painless. Yet again he had come home so late at night that you could almost call it early, and flopped into bed after another "ruff session" at the Bug Out Club where everybody knows him as Bad Bwoy MC John Wayne! "It was pure roadblock down there tonight, y'know Donna," he had explained sleepily, "and I had to work 'nuff-'nuff to set the crowd on fire. But me have some sweet loving for you in the morning, baby." Wayne was the kind of man who insisted that he didn't want no "downtown and no sixty-nine," no matter how much he loved his woman and his idea of hard work was rapping on a sound system every weekend. It made him feel massive and 'broad'. Big deal! He'd spend the rest of the week chewing on the end of a pencil, writing rhymes — that was overtime! So there he was 'working overtime', loafing, and there I was working as a waitress and bringing in the money. It all hit me in one go that night as he snored softly in the bed beside me — reeking of smoke and Dragon Stout. He was easily satisfied, while I was made for better things and was wasting my time hanging around the neighbourhood going nowhere. Contrary to popular belief, women are more quick to terminate a bad

45

relationship than men. I am a romantic realist and I knew then that I was going to London alone. The past year of my life flashed before my eyes like snapshots in a Kodak ad. Life with Wayne wasn't going to work out.

I had been all ready to move to London the previous year. I had met an agent who had said that she could get me work dancing in music videos. I knew that that wasn't going to make me rich, but at least I'd be in the right places, meeting the right people, rather than in Bristol twiddling my thumbs. But then I met Wayne — 'Mr Cool an' Deadly', or more appropriately 'Mr Mention' — 25-years-old and with skin as smooth as fine leather. He seemed exciting and wanted the same things as me.

'Love' is a woman's weakness and what I felt for Wayne at first was something close to it. He was the only one in the bar when he swaggered in that first time, mobile phone in one hand, and ordered a 'Blueberry Hill' in a cone. Maybe it was his seductive smile, maybe it was the twinkle in his eye; it's hard to look back on it now, but yeah, he had me weak at the knees. I dipped into the freezer for his order, he passed a few complimentary remarks, I told him to behave himself and we exchanged mischievous glances. Before I knew it, I was giving him my home number. Strictly sexual attraction, you understand. I wanted to sleep with him. I thought 'what the hell', I had a whole summer to kill in Bristol, I may as well enjoy it. That intimate summer together was the best we were gonna get. I got to know and like Wayne more each day he came into the bar for his 'Blueberry Hill' and in the evenings at the movies, in the quayside cafes and with me simply resting my head on his bare chest in his parked car in the woods overlooking the city. Sex of course was safe. Wayne was one hundred percent lust and lustful, he knew exactly how to give the agony and make it hurt so good.

He wanted to move to London in the New Year, he said, to try his luck in the music business. We decided that we would move to the capital together and gave ourselves six months to save up enough money to live there for a while, just in case we didn't get any work immediately. I worked two jobs and saved as much as I could. I even moved in with Wayne because it would be cheaper. Day after day I prodded him along, until he became dependent upon my proddings, *my* ideas and *my* dreams.

But while I saved, Wayne continued with his same lifestyle of deejaying at weekends and spending the money he earned through the week.

"Don't worry 'bout dat, baby," he replied every time I asked him how his saving was going. "Everyt'ing is taken care of."

Of course it wasn't. Wayne hadn't saved a penny. When it all came out in the open, he added that he wasn't all that bothered about going to London after all. If it happened it happened, but he was in no hurry, as certain things were happening for him in Bristol and he wouldn't mind hanging around waiting, if necessary.

"So why didn't you mention this before?" I asked angrily. "We've spent the last six months planning to move to London. You know what it means to me, and now you tell me that you're not bothered. Thanks for nothing, Wayne."

He tried to make out that he had only come to the conclusion recently, when he had considered that it was probably better to be a big fish in a small pond like Bristol than to try to compete with the millions of other people in London. "I need time to sort myself out," he said, which usually meant that he wanted an unspecified amount of time to carry on raving to his heart's desire and to 'deal' with any admiring females he came across on his travels.

The bottom line was that Wayne was scared of leaving the town he grew up in. If he had his way he would rarely leave the familiar surroundings of St. Paul's, let alone Bristol itself. That was where all his friends were and that was the place he called home and he was too afraid to disrupt his life so much by moving to the big city. I had to face the facts: while I was with Wayne, I would never get to London.

I'm not the kind of woman that hangs around waiting for something to happen. I'm independent, spontaneous and adventurous, when I see something I want to do, I go for it because no amount of dreaming is gonna get it. I want variety and excitement in my relationships and to make the most of my life. Whenever I made demands on our relationship Wayne would always reply in a whiny voice, "I'm too busy," "I'm too tired," "maybe next week," "I want to be romantic, but I'm just too forgetful."

I met Donald at a New Year's Eve party in Clifton where I was shocking out in a black wet-look shorts and blouse combination and a peroxide blonde wig. I looked at him and he looked at me and I knew right away that something was going to go down. We danced a couple of slow numbers together after which he coaxed me into the bathroom on the pretext that he had "something serious" to say. Inside, we stood kissing deeply and intently for several minutes. It was hardly a romantic setting, but we barely noticed when other partygoers banged on the door, trying to use the lavatory. He was an all right looker, but nothing special and I told him that I was "other people's property". He said he didn't mind, that we could be discreet and that behind closed doors nobody but us would know if we had an affair.

"I can take you places you ain't been before baby," he offered.

I told him that I was only interested in going to London and did he have a car? He said, 'fine' he could deal with that, and "My car is at your disposal."

By the end of the night, I had weakened. Donald lay the seduction on fast and thick and when you know that you're going home to an empty bed, it can succeed. We did it at his house, an unmemorable affair.

So when Wayne stumbled into bed yet again the next night, I made up my mind to call Donald early and tell him I was ready to go the following day. I scanned the classified pages of my latest copy of The Voice, checking out the 'accommodation offered' section.

Almost immediately, I regretted agreeing to drive to London with Donald. He pulled up in a Volkswagen Golf with a boom box and some mad mix tapes of all the latest junglist music.

"Nice car," I complimented.

"Yeah man," Donald replied, stroking the leather steering wheel, "nice, y'know."

We loaded my gear into the car. Wayne was sound asleep, his body not yet fully recharged after a night of passionate love, which unbeknown to him was to be our last. I left him a note without a forwarding address. I didn't want him coming looking for me. The whole point with this was that I was embarking on a new life, without him and I didn't want to be dragged back to the way we were, ever. I had to put feelings for Wayne aside so that my dreams could come true.

We hadn't driven very far down the motorway before

49

Donald started acting odd. His hand slipped from the gear shift onto my thigh. He gave my knee a gentle squeeze and flashed a toothy smile.

"I really enjoyed making love after that party," he said. "I'm looking forward to the next time."

He winked at me knowingly, then as if to get me in the mood, pushed a cassette of X-rated ragga music into the Golf's stereo system.

Having sex with him was a mistake, and it was simply not that good. I know what good sex is and that wasn't it. And as far as I could see, Donald had nothing else to offer me.

When it comes to love and sex I know what I want and how to get it. If you've got a positive attitude you'll attract partners. But you mustn't try too hard to find someone. If I was interested in Donald he wouldn't have had to ask:

"So how interested are you in me?"

I looked at the motorway ahead, it was still a long way to London. I leaned back on the head rest and let the Shabba bassline tickle the base of my spine before answering.

"Well, I'm looking forward to us becoming really close friends," I answered diplomatically. But that didn't satisfy Donald.

"Friends?" he echoed. "Forget dat... lovers is what we are."

He started moaning about black women, how they were dissing the brothers and how they had to stop it and start supporting them to the fullness instead of playing games and teasing and misusing. I began to fear that Donald would expect a payment 'in kind' for driving me to London. I had already given him enough money to cover the petrol and I now offered to take him out to lunch when we arrived.

"I don't want you having to go into debt just to treat me well," I said, but he didn't catch my drift.

"Don't worry," he replied his eyes fixed on the road, "I'm going to *nyam* my lunch when we get to London or before, take your pick," he said slapping my thigh hard and grinning to himself. He turned up the music some more as Shabba's voice came through the speakers singing *Mr Loverman*.

Donald thought he was smart when he turned off the motorway suddenly and pulled into a lay-by, so I had to play smarter. I reached in the back seat for my handbag.

"Before we have sex, do you mind if I change my tampax, you see I've been bleeding heavily all night long," I said, pulling out a box of tampons.

An expression of acute distaste came across his face. No longer down with 'gettin' down', he spun the steering wheel all the way round and with a screech of his tyres executed a hasty U-turn back to the motorway.

He was quiet for the rest of the journey, keeping his mind on the road and the sound of Chaka Demus and Pliers, which had replaced the x-rated stuff in the stereo system.

I had to diss him one more time however, when we arrived in London. He started talking his funny business again and said that he was going to come down the next week to check me for his 't'ing'. I told him that I didn't have an address, and lied that I would call him when I had one. But this time Donald wasn't going to be fobbed off. He said that he would keep my luggage and drive it back with him to Bristol until I called. My mind was ticking fast, how was I going to get out of this one? The last thing I wanted was this lunatic to have my new address in London. As we waited at a red traffic light, my salvation came in the form of a police car.

"I'll just ask these cops the way," I told Donald as I wound down my window.

"Excuse me officers," I called across, "we're from Bristol and we're a bit confused... We were told that you can drive in London with no MOT on your car, is that true?"

"What the fuck...?!" Donald began, but it was too late, the two police officers in the patrol car indicated that we should pull over to the side.

Donald obeyed meekly, cursing me under his breath, perspiration dripping from his hands and neck. I didn't waste any time. As the police checked the Volkswagen for road-worthiness, I climbed out and flagged down a passing cab and transferred my three suitcases from Donald's car.

"I told him those tyres were past the legal limit!"

I called out to the police as I hopped into the taxi, confident that I would never see Donald again.

NEW JACK SISTAS

The cab driver glanced in his rear view mirror at his elegant passenger. She looked nice too, he thought, checking her out. 'Yeah, I wouldn't mind a bite of that!' He hadn't even minded when she had asked if he would tune his radio out of his favourite jazz station to a soul station. That's how good she looked.

Dee sipped her pint-size bottle of Evian thoughtfully as the cab drove through the south London suburb of Wimbledon. She hadn't yet been to this part of town, but from what she could see of the quaint little Victorian cottages and the quiet tree-lined streets, it seemed pretty fashionable. Finally the taxi pulled up outside a house in the middle of a terrace of grey-bricked dwellings. Dee peered out of the window briefly and checked the number. Yes, this was it. She paid the driver, telling him to "keep the change" and climbed out.

Carol switched off the vacuum cleaner and waited, listening. The door bell ding-donged its familiar chime again. She unplugged the Hoover and shoved it hurriedly into the cupboard under the staircase and rushed to the door.

"Hi!"

"You must be Dee," Carol said, briefly studying the business-suited woman with the 'ring of confidence' smile on her doorstep.

"That's right... and of course you're Carol. I am so pleased to meet you," Dee said, stretching out her hand.

Carol led the way into the house.

"Let me show you around upstairs first," she said and made her way up, the visitor close behind her.

"Mmmmn...!" Dee uttered as Carol opened the door to the spacious bedroom she intended to rent out. The room was immaculate, with a spotless, fitted, white lambswool carpet and painted white walls with a subtle hint of yellow. In the centre was a double bed and to one side a dressing table. The dark green velvet curtains hung down to the carpet.

Dee fell in love with the room immediately. Carol took her through the rest of the house, to the upstairs study and the bathroom, then back down to the split-level open plan living room and the kitchen to the side and the little refectory at the back overlooking the large garden.

"I'll take it," Dee said eagerly as she stood in the conservatory, she didn't need to see any more.

Carol smiled. The American woman seemed nice but before she would allow anybody to move into her room she wanted to know a lot more about them. She decided that they may as well sit in the conservatory and drink some iced tea while she went over the references and they both got to know each other.

Dee eased herself into the other wicker chair, a broad smile across her face.

"This place is really nice... believe me. I've been looking at a lot of places, but this is the best I've seen, I've got good vibes about this place already, " she said.

"So which part of the States are you from?" Carol asked, pouring out two glasses of iced tea from the decanter on the glass-topped wicker table beside her and offering a slice of home made double chocolate cake.

Dee had a small slice.

"Oh I'm really from Baton Rouge, Louisiana, but I've lived in Chicago for about seven years. I guess now you could say I'm from the mid-west."

"Chicago!" Carol said with a glint of recognition. "Al Capone... the Untouchables..."

"Please honey," Dee retorted in an overstated southern drawl and pointing a disapproving finger at her hostess. "Ain't nobody in Chicago 'untouchable' and the only Al Capone I know owns the local deli on my block."

The two women exchanged a few chuckles as they sipped their glasses of iced tea.

"And how do you find London?" Carol asked.

"Oh it's a beautiful city, no really. The buildings are so old and there are lots of really quaint places to visit... I just love Buckingham Palace. But you know what, with the work I do I haven't really been able to meet too many black folk. I'm in advertising, I work for an English company and most of the people I meet seem to be of the 'caucasian persuasion'."

"So let me ask you a question," Dee said. "Why are you renting out the room?"

"My husband walked out and left me. I need the money."

"Oh I'm sorry," Dee said quickly, surprised at her hostess' frankness, "it's really none of my business."

"That's alright. It's not a big deal... I read somewhere that two out of every three black marriages end in divorce, so I shouldn't have been surprised after seven years. I'm not bitter about it anymore; it's probably the best thing that has happened to me in years. Eight wasted years with him. Have you ever been married?"

Dee shook her head.

"Lucky you. All the things I could have done if I hadn't married... I don't care who you are, men get the best deal out of marriage, because becoming a husband is better than becoming somebody's wife. Well at least I'll never again have to look at another dirty pair of men's briefs in the laundry basket! That's why I specifically requested a female flatmate in the advert, I've had enough of men."

Dee regretted bringing the subject up. Even though Carol made light of it there was a sombre edge to her voice. Maybe she could do with a friendly ear, Dee thought.

"He left you for another woman, right?"

"Yes, his secretary — blonde hair and blue eyes, long legs, big tits, you know the score."

"Jungle fever!" Dee remarked with a sigh. "Another brother with a white woman. What's the deal with all this inter-racial dating anyway? In the short time I've been in England it's seems like half the brothers I see are dating white women. You see a lot more of that here than in the States."

"Who knows," Carol said contemplatively. "I've heard all kinds of explanation, that white women give them an easy time..."

"Please!" Dee cried out, raising her hand to say 'enough'. "I ain't falling for that tired old talk, girlfriend. Nobody's as easy on the black man as the sisters and when we ask in return for a little respect, the next thing we know they're running after some white woman because of all the pressure!"

The two women laughed, enjoying the joke together.

"The hardest thing about becoming single again," Carol said reflectingly, "is that you waste so much time pondering the relationship you don't get anything done. I know it's wrong, but it's like my husband's still got his claws in me. I don't even want to think about him and yet he's right there, everywhere I turn."

"Ungh-ungh!" Dee disagreed. "Not me chile. I've got better things to do with my time than think about my ex.

'Cause he's history and I've gotta keep on movin'. Let me tell you something, since I broke up with my man I've been going places, 'cause I shut him out and focused on my career. That's what you've got to do."

From what Dee had seen, black women in Britain shared the same problems and the same desires as their counterparts in the States.

"Whatever the situation, you must admit that black men come up with some lame-ass excuses," Dee continued, pouring herself another glass of iced tea. "My ex in Chicago had some good ones... Things never worked out between us. Yeah, he was a good looker and he had potential, but he wanted me to make all kinds of big concessions. His favourite excuse was, 'You know, it's difficult to have a true intimate relationship as a black man, we're already so exposed'."

Carol agreed that it was a good one and they both laughed. She found herself at ease with this American woman and could tell that they would have a lot of fun together if she moved in. She decided to offer Dee the room, when the doorbell chimed again.

"Hi, I'm Donna!"

Carol stood looking puzzled at the muffin-brown skinned woman standing on her doorstep in some impossibly high-heels, dressed in a flimsy black bell bottoms and a minuscule white blouse.

"Can I help you?"

"It's me, Donna..." the girl said blinking her large, bright eyes excitedly and flashing a million dollar smile, in between chewing gum, rapidly. "The advert... remember, I called up yesterday to see the room."

Carol had completely forgotten that she had invited another woman to view the room. She looked the younger woman up and down. She certainly had her own distinct dress style and was the type of woman that would get noticed wherever she went. Anyone could see that judging by appearances the two women had little in common.

"I'm sorry, but the room has just gone."

Donna's disappointment was clear from the expression on her face.

"But you said that you wouldn't make your decision until everyone had been in to see it."

Carol had forgotten that also. She felt uncomfortable, but what could she do? She had made her decision and she didn't want to waste Donna's time.

"I'm sorry," she said, there didn't seem to be anything else to add.

"But I've come all the way from Bristol just to see the flat."

"Oh no... I didn't know that... I'm so sorry."

Carol started feeling bad about it. She hadn't promised the woman anything and she really had intended to vet all the applicants first but she already knew that Dee was the flat mate she was going to choose. Frankly, Donna's flamboyant style and the difference in their ages were not going to influence her decision.

"Look, I've just made a jug of iced tea, why don't you come in to get your thoughts together."

Dejectedly, Donna followed Carol into the house balancing herself precariously on her high heels with every step.

"Oh this place is just perfect!" said Donna, looking around her at the luscious living room and through to the conservatory beyond.

"Hi, I'm Dee," the American said, offering her hand. She had overheard the doorstep exchange. Donna's arrival had placed her in an uncomfortable position.

"I'm afraid there's been a mix up," Carol explained, "I was telling Donna here that you've just beaten her to the room, but unfortunately she's come a long way."

"A hundred and twenty miles!" Donna stressed.

"I thought she was in London," Carol said, trying to joke, but it wasn't funny and they all knew it.

"It is such a shame," Donna said, looking around as she sat down on one of the cushioned wicker armchairs, "I've got a feeling about this place... it's just right."

"That's exactly what I said," Dee offered, sympathetically.

"So you've moved to London?" Carol asked.

"Yeah, today... Been trying to for about a year.. finally you know... just left... best way... don't think about it, just go..."

"Before you came in we were talking about our 'men'," Dee said.

"What do you mean the lack of them?" Donna asked.

"Well at least you come from a country that has men like Blair Underwood, Denzel Washington and Larry Fishburne," Carol turned to Dee.

"Well those guys aren't exactly standing on every street corner," Dee said with a laugh. "Believe me, I've looked. And if I did find one of them, I certainly wouldn't be kicking him out of my bed!"

They laughed and each woman admitted that they would see nothing wrong with a little bumping and grinding with Wesley.

"Every woman should get at least one chance in her life to actually meet a man like Wesley," Donna added.

Neither Dee nor Carol could see anything wrong with that either.

Carol had begun to like Donna. The younger woman

59

seemed bright and cheerful. Maybe she would be fun to have as a flatmate.

"You know what you should do with this place," Donna continued, "I would get rid of the carpet in the living room... What have you got under there, floorboards? Yeah well, I would sand down the floorboards and polish them with some clear varnish and that would make a wicked living room."

"Do you think so?" Carol asked. She had considered doing the very same thing, but had never got around to it.

"So isn't there even just one more room in this house?" Donna asked changing the subject to more pressing matters. "I mean, I wouldn't take up very much room. I'm quite small really, I just look tall, that's all... I mean, I'll be honest, I'm desperate, I was kind of counting on seeing this place and giving you a deposit. I've got nowhere else to go."

Carol looked amazed at Donna. How could she have depended on getting just this flat? Dee said that she had relied just as heavily on getting the flat after seeing the ad in The Voice, just because it sounded right. Carol began to feel guilty again.

"I mean," Donna continued, "I could even just use this living room, or this conservatory as my room. I could get a little mattress, which I'd fold up every morning and fold out late at night after everybody's gone to bed."

Carol didn't need to think about that one. It was definitely not a good idea

"Look, I feel really responsible about this whole thing," Dee offered. "I don't know how you feel about this Carol, it's your house, but I don't mind sharing my room with Donna at all."

Carol shook her head. No that wasn't necessary.

60

"Why are you so desperate for somewhere to live?"

"I had to leave Bristol. I was in a relationship which wasn't going anywhere, with a worthless man. It was stifling me, being stuck with a man without ambition, who couldn't see that I needed more... Where's your black man when you want some emotional support, eh?"

"Well, what's a real man?" Carol asked. Men think they know, but they can't define it."

"A real man," Dee began, "is a responsible person who can stand alone if necessary, a man who can be warm, comforting and kind, a person who doesn't need to prove his masculinity all the time, a man who doesn't give his penis too much attention, because that means he gives his woman too little attention."

"You can't cure a cocks man," Donna added.

"I know exactly what you mean," Dee said pouring out some more tea. "A lot of black men hate to admit it, but hey, the truth is the truth! Sometimes I think that the only reason I don't act like the men do, is that a woman in my position doesn't get many chances to do so."

The three women talked like this for a couple of hours, like long time friends unaware of the hours ticking away. They all agreed that the implications of falling in love quickly was more complicated for women and that while the men were big on the 'love at first sight' syndrome, they as conscious black women owed it to themselves not to fall for the same old 'flim-flam'. Finally Carol decided that there was just one way for *both* of her new-found friends to move in. She turned to Donna:

"There is one more room, but it's tiny. It's used as a study at the moment, but we can move the books and computer. How would you feel about that?"

"Believe me, that would be just fine," Donna insisted. "All I need is a wardrobe size room and I'm happy."

Carol smiled and took Donna upstairs to view the room. The younger woman said that it looked great and they shook hands on it immediately.

"I really have to thank you for this," Donna said. "I don't know what I would have done otherwise. Do you mind if I move in later on this evening?"

"That's alright," Carol said, "I could do with the extra rent money anyway. I have got a good feeling about this. I'm sure that we're all going to become great friends."

Dee and Donna agreed and they toasted their future together with a glass of chilled white wine from the bottle Carol had kept in the refrigerator for the right occasion.

INDECENT PROPOSAL

One of the first things I need to know when I meet a man, is his relationship with his penis. Men regard their sexual organs much too seriously because it's the only childhood toy they get to keep and play with for their entire life. The penis is a man's best friend because it never deserts him, even when his woman's left him. That's why a lot of men are willing to risk everything they have, everything they've built up — their career and their home and family — all for the sake of a penis.

I soon realised that mine was the only black face in the Croydon offices of Splash Advertising. Even as I was shown around the building on my first day I caught a couple of guys nudge each other, leering at me in an explicitly sexual manner. That was the one chance I was going to allow. If it came to it I was prepared to show them that this was one sister who could take care of herself.

I had no trouble fitting into the company. I had got the job as creative director, which was basically the same as what I was doing for Frazier Clarke in Chicago, handling equally large accounts. The salary was good and so were the working conditions in a large, bright, fifth floor open-plan office. I had no complaints about the job or the department, except that there were no black people in the company. Every now and then a black motorcycle courier dropped in to pick up some artwork, but apart from that I was on my own.

I have never felt so isolated as I felt in those first two

63

weeks in London when I was still living in a hotel. I would go to Splash every morning and come back to an empty hotel room every evening, with no one to offload onto, no one I could relate with. A couple of times I even went out with some of the people from the office when they asked me to, but it wasn't the same. At the end of happy hour I would take a cab home to my hotel room, with an empty heart to spend another evening alone. Even though I had become friends with Helen, one of the receptionists, who was always suggesting that I should go out 'raving' with her on the weekends, I wasn't really enjoying myself or meeting the kind of people I wanted to meet. Helen wanted to go downtown to the pubs in Covent Garden. That was her idea of having a good time, but it wasn't mine, so I came up with excuses to make sure that our social contacts ended after work.

"A lot of women wish they were in your shoes... They'd like to have your looks, your chances in life, your job, the way you attract men... and you're complaining!"

"But where are all the black folk?"

Julian Phillips was too typically British to understand where I was coming from, but when he asked me if I was enjoying working for the company and I told him straight that I was disappointed not to see at least one or two other black faces.

He was young for an account executive but somehow he seemed older than his years and he always liked to give the impression that he wasn't just in charge of the department but also always available to give advice on domestic problems. I didn't know if I actually liked him, especially after I caught a glimpse of him admiring my behind. I decided to let that one go for now. Mostly though I didn't like Julian because he seemed shallow and self-centred and as far as I had gathered in the two weeks of working under him, he didn't seem to have good professional judgment. He was employed to explain agency thinking to the client and client thinking to the agency and to act as a focal point for the agency's activities, but he saw his job more as one of an agony uncle, always offering to "lend an ear or a friendly word of advice" on any personal issues and to only occasionally mastermind a brilliant ad campaign and keep the account profitable. He always seemed to be wandering around the office, praising everyone because things were going so well. But on the few occasions when he was genuinely needed he never seemed to be around.

One afternoon he offered to drive me around to some of the more 'ethnic' areas in London after work. I only had an empty bed waiting for me in the hotel room so I accepted. We drove around in his new model dark green Jaguar, cruising around areas like Brixton, Peckham, Battersea and Streatham. Even checking out everywhere from the comfort of the leather front passenger seat, I could tell that these were neighbourhoods I would feel much more at ease in than in the areas I had been frequenting.

We decided to stop at a brasserie in Brixton for a drink. Julian said that I would like the place and he was right. In the two weeks I had been in London it was the first time I was able to go to a place where there was an abundance of elegantly dressed black men and women who looked like they were going places. I made a note of the address and vowed to myself to return at some point, without Julian.

"I've been out with a few black women, you know," Julian shouted over the music from the loudspeakers.

Big deal... Am I supposed to be grateful that he has graced

Black Womankind with his presence?

I was still sipping on my half-empty glass of white wine, Julian was on his second or third beer.

"Yes, I consider myself an 'equal opportunity dater'," he said with a self-assured smile.

I think I'm going to throw up!

"...I've noticed one thing," he continued, "my black dates seem to dress better and are less frequently overweight than my white dates. Now why do you think that's the case?"

I told him that it didn't surprise me.

"And it's funny," he continued, "I've known black women who weren't earning that much, spending half their salary every week on getting their hair done."

What does he know?

"Is that so?" I responded. I mean, it wasn't like he was telling me something I didn't already know

"So how do you really like your job with Splash? Come on now, you can be frank, it's off the record. Don't think of me as your boss."

I looked around me in the brasserie, at the young black couples in his and hers Karl Kani 'college' outfits, sitting whispering sweet nothings to each other over bottles of wine. I sipped at my drink. Yes, I could tell Julian exactly what I thought about the job, but then again, he wouldn't understand.

"I like it, I am really enjoying myself. I'm having a great time being in London and the people at Splash are cool, I've met some really nice people."

I stopped before I got caught in my own exaggeration. Julian smiled.

"I'm sure you're going to be very happy at Splash and I am sure that we are going to be very happy with you."

He touched my hand gently, whether reassuringly or

otherwise, I didn't know but I didn't like it.

"You'll find us very reasonable," he continued, catching the waiter's eye and indicatingthat he wanted another beer, "and you'll find me very fair. I don't expect much..." he laughed, thinking about it.

Julian seemed surprised that as a black woman I was more attracted to black men than to him. I told him that it wasn't a political thing, it was just a preference. The days when marrying white was seen as a stepping stone to social advancement are long over, I explained. Now white men have to compete with black men on equal terms and I hadn't yet met a white man who appealed to me enough to date, that was all.

As the time drew on, Julian became more and more informal and started talking loosely. Had he been entirely sober he probably wouldn't have given me such a good insight into his personal scheming and dealing. Far from discouraging him I let him talk, picking up any pieces of information that I could along the way. He boasted a lot about being good at his job and so determined that he would deliberately lose at a game of golf, just to get an account.

"That's how it is out there in the real world," he said proudly. "Forget all this politically correct stuff and the proper way to do these things, it's dog eat dog out there and I don't intend to be pet food for anybody. That's why I'm trying to set up my own agency. And when I do... No, not 'if', *when* I do, I might just take you along," he promised, with an unsober expression on his face.

The time must have whizzed by, because suddenly it was 11.30pm. It was when I looked at my watch that I noticed Julian's head nodding off briefly.

"Are you alright?" I asked.

He hiccoughed and said he was fine, but he clearly

wasn't. I thought he had only had three or four beers plus the liquor shots, but the waiter told me it was eight! Damn, the last thing I wanted was my drunk boss on my hands, and how was I going to get back to my hotel? He was in no condition to drive his Jaguar.

To be honest, I was pissed at having to accompany him in the cab. Julian had fallen asleep by now and the driver said he wouldn't take him unless I went along. What could I do? I sighed and pushed Julian into the car and climbed in after him. I managed to wake him sufficiently to find out his address, before he nodded back to sleep for the entire journey.

It was already midnight when the cab pulled up outside the new development of apartments at Surrey Docks where Julian lived in a penthouse apartment overlooking the River Thames. I told the driver to wait for me as I helped Julian in, using the keys in his pocket. It wasn't as easy as I thought. Julian was a tall man and it took all my strength to pull, push, drag and coax him up the three flights of steps. All those extra weight training sessions I had been doing in keep-fit had a practical use after all. Inside, the apartment was immaculate, with pale blue carpets throughout that looked like they'd never been walked over, pale blue walls that looked like they had been recently decorated and a television, stereo and other furniture which looked like they had been unpacked the day before. I wasn't interested in all that anyway and got out of there the moment Julian flopped lifelessly on his bed, throwing his house keys on the coffee table in his living room on the wa outy.

I could have only been gone a few minutes, but downstairs, the cab driver had disappeared. Damn! I looked all around, the streets were deserted. There wasn't a single car in sight. Behind me I could hear the river waves lapping softly, but otherwise there was silence. I walked around in different directions, hoping to find a payphone or some semblance of life to direct me to a cab, but nothing. Julian seemed to live in the middle of nowhere. Eventually I traced my footsteps back to his apartment building and buzzed on his entryphone. I must have been buzzing for three or four minutes before he eventually answered, sounding jacked.

"Julian, buzz me up, it's Dee."

"Dee? Oh, Dee, come up."

The buzzer went and the door clicked open.

"What happened?" he asked dazed as I reached the top of the stairs. He was dressed exactly as I had left him in his crumpled grey suit, white shirt and loosened tie.

"I couldn't get a cab," I said stiffly, trying to contain my anger at being compromised into this situation.

"You'll have to stay here," he said with a concerned look on his face, still reeking of alcohol.

That didn't seem to me to be a good idea at all. He gave me some numbers and I tried phoning for a cab, but it was the same answer everywhere, I would have to wait about an hour.

"Look, trust me, you can stay here," Julian insisted, yawning. "You can sleep in the bedroom and I'll sleep here on the sofa."

I had heard lines like that before. Every time a man says 'trust me', alarm bells start ringing in my head. I weighed up my chances, but realised that I didn't have much choice. I was tired and I didn't know the area well enough to take my chances on the cold, dark, quiet streets outside.

Julian gave me a night shirt and a toothbrush and towel. I washed my face in the bathroom. I was too tired to think of anything but sleep and soon flopped on his ample bed with its satin sheets.

I must have dozed off quickly, because the next thing I knew, I was woken up by Julian — standing butt naked over me, about to climb into the bed. A scrawny white body ambling towards me with his manhood standing to attention in front of him! I kicked out quickly, reflexively and before I knew it, he was bent double on the carpet, clutching his crutch and groaning with pain. I think he got the message, because he crawled back into the living room and didn't try it again for the rest of the night. The next morning, I woke up early as the sun streamed through the bedroom window. I got up, dressed, got my things together and tiptoed through the living room where Julian was wheezing lightly through a deep slumber, then slipped out of the door without waking him.

I went to my hotel in town and freshened up, before taking a train out to Croydon. I got to work late and to my surprise, my office had a different name on its door.

"What's going on?" I asked Helen.

"I could ask you the same thing, Dee. I got a call from Julian when I got in, telling me that you had to swap offices. Something about a mix up."

She pointed to a tiny office across the hall. I was fuming. My things had all been transferred to the smaller room, which was also the darkest spot in the office with no windows.

"Where is he?" I asked, ready for war..

"Oh, he's not in yet."

"Well honey, as soon as he steps through that door, you let me know."

There was nothing I could do but wait. If Julian was smart he wouldn't play with me like this. I hadn't come all the way from the States to be messed about by him or

70

anybody else."

Julian kept a low profile for the rest of the day. I didn't really feel like working too much either. Not until this 'mix up' had been resolved. So I simply sat in my 'cupboard' with a blank sheet of paper, trying to come up with a new ad line for a particular campaign.

I waited for him the next day also, but he still didn't show. By the time he dragged his sorry ass in on the third day, I was ready for him.

He stopped talking to his colleague and had a tense look on his face as he saw me approaching. I cornered him by the entrance. I didn't waste words and demanded an immediate explanation as to why I had been moved out of my office. In a typically stiff upper-lip British manner, he suggested that we should discuss the matter in his office. I followed him in.

"I must say that I'm disappointed in you, Dee. As your superior, I really must insist that you address me in a much more formal way while we're at work."

"Forget that bullshit," I cut in impatiently, "let's just get to the point. Why have I been moved to that shoe box out there?"

I was steaming, the anger had been boiling up in me for two days and at that precise moment I didn't care if I got fired. I was ready for the worst.

"As I explained to Helen, there's been a mix up," he said. "When I looked through the schedules I noticed that your office had already been aquisitioned for someone else. Oh I do apologise," he said with overstated irony.

I looked at him hard, his eyes were laughing at me. He knew and I knew that it wasn't about that, so why didn't he come out with it straight?

"So all of this, is because you couldn't make it with me the other night, isn't it?"

"As I said," he answered defensively, "it's all an unfortunate mix up."

His eyes laughed at me again.

"Let's cut the bullshit," I said eventually, calming down a touch. "There's nobody else here but me and you, just let me know where I stand."

"If you must know, you've got to learn that it pays to keep your superiors happy."

"So what are you trying to say, just give it to me straight, if I had let you have sex with me the other night, I would still be in my original office?"

Julian smiled now that it was getting through to me.

"Exactly!"

"And if I keep you 'happy', my time here will be happy?"

He smiled again.

"I think you're getting the picture," he said, moving behind me and caressing my shoulders slowly with his hands. "And if I'm not happy, you won't be happy, because you'll be without a job and without your job you'll lose your work permit."

I turned around and pushed him off my shoulders. I had got what I wanted, now Julian was gonna get his.

I went all the way to the top man, the managing director, who agreed to see me after a few minutes. I pulled out the tape recorder and played the tape. The old man almost choked on his cigar. He didn't need to hear more, he knew what the implication was. He buzzed his secretary and asked her to call their lawyers immediately. The lawyers arrived after an hour, by which time Julian had been summoned. He didn't know what was going on, but when he saw me he guessed and decided to go on the offensive.

"I was going to let you know as soon as possible,

Morris," he addressed the managing director, "that with regret I was forced to sack Ms Robinson earlier today for gross misconduct."

"Don't worry about that Julian, you've been working too hard, much too hard." The old man patted Julian on the shoulders like an understanding friend. "We're going to be sending you on holiday, for a long while. There's a good chap."

I looked across at Julian almost pitifully. There was no need to gloat about my victory, he was leaving and I was staying, that was enough for me.

SCREWFACE

Carol looked on enviously as a typical 'black family for the nineties' passed her by in the fruit section of her local Tesco supermarket. The man looked proud pushing a trolley laden with food, with a new-born baby in the pouch on his back and a little girl at his side sucking her thumb and hanging on to her father with her other hand, while the woman checked her list as she selected the week's provisions. That was how it should be, Carol thought, that was all she had ever wanted. Surely she had as much right as anyone else to a loving relationship?

Going to the supermarket every Friday evening had become one of the highlights of Carol's week. The rent money meant she could once again buy little luxuries like crab meat, fresh pasta and smoked salmon. Since her sister Janice had said that supermarkets had become a popular meeting place for singles — giving the opportunity to make visual contact several times without commitment or even verbal contact — Carol had half-seriously kept one eye alert for any 'action' in between the fresh pasta and the baked beans. Her eyes scanned the aisles furtively, expecting to see couples exchanging phone numbers and arranging dates, but to no avail.

"You have to shop at the same stores, at the same time, and you'll meet the same people." At this time there were always men popping in to the supermarket for groceries on their return from work and from the amount of food they had in their shopping baskets, they were cooking for one only. Apparently laundrettes and bookshops also offered good opportunities for meeting single black men, but Carol was really quite happy sleeping alone.

As she stood in the queue at the check-out, Carol felt a pair of eyes staring across at her from the next check-out. She tried to ignore it, but the back of her neck was burning.

She turned eventually to see who it was. A tall, dark-skinned, average-looking, thirty-something man in a grey-pinstripe suit smiled at her warmly. She thought she recognised the face from way back in her past.

"Carol, isn't it?" he called across. "You don't remember me, do you? Kelvin, Michelle's brother... Michelle Johnson, Hornsey Girls, remember?"

Of course, a blast from her school days past. It must have been twenty years at least. She remembered Kelvin, Michelle's older brother. When you are fourteen, you readily give your heart to sixteen year old boys. As she recalled, she had a secret childhood crush on him. Had she not years later thought about him and wished, "If only I could meet him today?"

Kelvin helped her to the car park with her shopping and after loading the carrier bags into the back of Carol's Escort, stood chatting and recalling the old days for a while.

"So how are you?"

"Fine," Carol said, nodding with a smile, "really fine."

"Yeah, I remember now," Kelvin recalled, "didn't you once have a crush on me?"

"Did I?" Carol said, feigning ignorance.

"Yeah, I think I remember my sister saying that, she said it was secret and I wasn't to let on."

"Are you sure about that?! I'm sure I would have remembered if it was a crush."

"Yeah, it was definitely a crush," Kelvin recalled

rubbing his chin with a big smile on his face.

He explained that he was now a pensions salesman and that he was doing it for the money which was really good.

"So how are you?" he asked again.

"Fine."

"And how is your boyfriend, or do I remember somebody saying that you got married? How is your husband?"

Carol lied and said fine.

"What a pity," Kelvin said with overstated disappointment. "I was hoping that I could invite you out some time. I don't suppose your husband would appreciate another man inviting his wife out to dinner?"

Kelvin fished around for any sign of interest from Carol but found nothing.

"No he wouldn't," she said.

She gave Kelvin no room for manoeuvre and waved goodbye to him as she drove out of the car park, without having exchanged numbers.

Marriage had proved to be a disappointing fantasy for Carol, even though she had tried hard to make it work.

She had not even found Neville that attractive during the year they were at college together. She had even kept her distance when he sought to begin a relationship with her. Though they didn't always agree and had fundamental differences of opinion on money, religion and politics — he wanted to raise Junior as 'black British' while she wanted to raise their son as 'African-Caribbean' — they enjoyed each other's company and had fun together at times when they weren't worrying about their son. They gave each other plenty of space and the relationship offered them both time to relax and chill out.

But after Junior died, everything changed. Neville's

personality became like a huge iceberg, with so much lying beneath his skin. They seldom went out together and when they did he openly flirted with other women.

Junior's death had brought Carol close to the face of death. It had made her realise that the one important thing in life was love. No matter how Neville behaved, Carol had been emotionally tied to him because of the son they had shared. If anything, she now loved him more deeply to fill the emptiness of their joint loss. She tried to be everything he wanted her to be and made sure she said "I love you," to him first thing in the morning and last thing at night. He was hurting too, he also needed healing. By the time she had accepted that she had become irrelevant to a large part of his life. She felt too old to become a single woman again, so she kept up the 'happily ever after' pretence to friends, family and herself.

Nobody said marriage was going to be easy, but she and Neville had known so many couples who had managed to make it work, who had learned the ability of making it through thick and thin, together for richer and for poorer and stayed happy. She was a fool, but she still believed that she was going to spend the rest of her life with Neville.

It was hard to suddenly go from spending every night for eight years with someone to being on your own, but nothing was worse for someone who had just been abandoned than blues; during the day when she was alone in the house, Carol would lie on the living room sofa playing her Billie Holiday until it made her cry. Who feels it knows it, and Billie *knew* it, her mournful voice the echo of a thousand shattered dreams, a million broken hearts. Like Billie, Carol knew that she had to forget her no good man and pretend that he had never existed, but she couldn't help flicking through their wedding album, trying to relive the memories of the good times. At least she had got the house.

After the episode at his office, Neville didn't want to have anything more to do with his wife and he got his lawyers to begin severing all links. He was only too eager to accept her lawyers' demand for the house to be transferred to her name and for papers to be quickly drawn up for an out of court settlement. He was flush with money because his company had offered its employees extremely generous bonuses according to profits going up. That year the bank's profits were so much higher than expected that a few of its employees had become millionaires overnight. Neville's bonus had enabled him to pay off the mortgage on their house, thereby softening the effect of the transfer of the deeds into his wife's name.

Despite agreeing to sign, Carol's bitterness had not subsided. Every hour of the day, her mind reverted back to Christmas Eve and to how Neville had abandoned her when she had needed him most and to the things he had said which could never be forgiven. She had plenty of time in between watching daytime classic films on the television and munching bags of crisps to work through her aggression, hate and sadness but she only had half a bottle of rum left to do it with. Food filled an empty space in her life and those culinary skills which she had gained as a housewife now helped her through the dark moments.

Neville had destroyed her faith in the black man by his lying and cheating and insensitivity and by his willingness to use their son's death as an excuse for his own infidelity. At first she was consumed by revenge, constantly planning how she was going to make his life a misery, the way he had destroyed her life. But the more she wasted time plotting revenge, the more she felt that Neville was still in control of her life. What she had to do was to explore her options. Like Kelvin, why had she not encouraged him? Even as she rejected his advances out of hand, Carol wished that she hadn't. Dinner with an old 'flame' would have been just what the psycho-analyst 'ordered' after the way Neville had abandoned her. But as much as she needed the healing, her memory told her that her life depended on not deepening the wound. Too many men interpreted 'dinner' as 'oral sex' for her to take the chance. Her hurt had been so deep that she would have to re-learn how to love.

Carol woke up in a passionate sweat. It had been so long since she had slept with a man. But that wasn't what she wanted in her life either. She was still young and there were countless things she wanted to do. She would deal with being single by engaging in other activities. She could adopt a child on her own or go back to school part-time. She would continue her work with the sickle cell support group which had helped her so much during Junior's suffering. A friend had asked her to review films for the local newspaper and Carol had to admit that she had become something of an 'expert' recently. She would earn some money and go on trips to Africa and Asia, or out to dinner or to the theatre. She would have any hairstyle she wanted, after all she no longer had a partner to stand and criticise it if he didn't like it. She would improve her physical appearance by shedding those extra pounds she'd been gradually putting on for the last few years and which she had always intended to get rid of. She would learn a foreign language and even learn to play the guitar, just for fun. She would visit that old school friend living in Birmingham she hadn't seen for quite some time and visit family and friends more regularly. She would write a dozen long over due letters every morning before doing anything else. And she would pamper herself with small luxuries. Her only regret now was that she had spent so many years with Neville, whilst her biological clock was ticking away like a time bomb. Never again, she vowed, would she stay in a relationship with someone who no longer liked her.

She had suspected that something was going on for months before Neville admitted it. He stopped asking her how her day had been and they no longer made love, for while she sat in bed needing a hug, Neville snored in Junior's room. While he slept, she went through his diary, sniffed at his shirts and switched on his computer, looking for clues that would confirm her suspicions of his infidelity. She found nothing, not even after going through the counterfoils in his cheque book.

She came within an inch of throwing everything away and having an affair herself. It was the summer, after they'd been fighting a lot. Neville was away on business, and Carol thought, 'What the hell, I'm going to a bar to see if I can get lucky."

As she was preparing to head out for the evening she removed her wedding ring. It took her nearly five minutes to do it. As she fought with the gold band, it occurred to her that she had never had that ring off her finger in all the time that she had been married. She stood in the doorway holding the ring, before going back inside believing that her marriage was worth more than a casual affair.

BOOPSIE

Men don't see nothing wrong with a little bump 'n' grind unless their woman's doing the bumping and another man's doing the grinding. But hey, I just wanna have fun. I'm in London and I'm having a fantastic time. I've landed on my feet, with a great place to live, earning just enough as a waitress and it's that time of year — Spring — when women come out to play. I'm not gonna turn down so many offers from men who want to do"anything" for me.

I didn't really want to live with two women in case they felt a way about me having several partners at the same time, or even one after the other. A lot of women can't handle someone who can jump in and out of relationships at the toss of a coin. But Dee and Carol are cool and pretty much get on with their own lives and don't mind me getting on with mine.

What's a girl to do? Everywhere I go some guy toots his car horn and offers to give me a lift or carry my bag. Every time I go raving, bouncers chat me up in the queue then just wave me through without paying. All of this happens because I like to dress in a way that attracts men, not for their money but more for what they can do for me.

Alex is as close to a 'boyfriend' as I've got. The others are just casual flings, but Alex is a real buddy.

We met at a house party up in Hampstead. A bunch of us piled into two cars after work one Saturday night at Corrina's, the Clapham Common restaurant I wait tables in. Someone knew of the party and the rest of us just followed. Inside the expansive house at the top of Haverstock Hill, four different sounds played on separate floors — junglist in the basement, soul on the ground floor, ragga on the first floor and rap on the top floor. The place was live and so were the people. Alex had gone there with some of his arty friends. He was doing a fine arts graduate course at the Royal College of Arts in Kensington and he was dressed suitably artistically in a purple denim 'Mao' jacket with a back to front baseball cap crowning his head. His dancing was as sensitive as his nature. While everybody else bopped to the ragga in rowdy fashion, Alex sort of flowed with the bass line to a rhythm that was not from the speakers but in his head.

We shared a rum and coke out in the chilly darkness of the garden and our joking somehow developed into a challenge to see who could come up with the best insult jokes:

"Your boyfriend's so ugly his doctor is a vet," Alex threw in.

"Your sister's so stupid I told her it was chilly outside, so she ran out with a knife and fork."

"Your boyfriend's so stupid he tripped over a cordless phone."

"Your brother's so ugly when he sits in the sand the cat tries to bury him."

"You're so stupid, on the job application where it said 'sign here' you wrote 'Aquarius'."

We fell about laughing and tickled each other playfully. When it came to be time to go, it was clear to me that I was going to spend the night at Alex's Brixton flat. It wasn't clear to him though and he stuttered for a moment, before getting the courage to suggest it.

His flat on the top floor of a four storey Victorian house on Landor Road, was small enough but seemed extra tiny because he shared it with Leo, another black artist from the RCA. Everywhere you looked there were huge paintings of stunning African women with proud expressions on their faces. Those were Leo's stuff, Alex explained, handing me a mug of Ovaltine. I had only half-finished my mug before we were in a passionate embrace on his mattress.

I know what good sex is, believe me. I don't always have the time to drop everything and enjoy sex like I'd want to, because I live such a hectic life. Enjoying sex is being happy just cuddling up to a lover and falling asleep in each other's arms. But most of the sex I was getting was just a case of 'in out, in out, and shake it all about'.

I know that the way we made love, Alex had never experienced the like before and because it was so satisfying to him I knew that I had the power of influence over him.

It wasn't just because it took him until the morning to recover, but because he confirmed it afterwards, between gasps of air as he lay on his back, my head cradled in his arm. He hadn't had too many sexual experiences, he confessed and he certainly hadn't had to work that hard before. He promised that he would run up Brixton Hill every morning to build up the stamina he was going to need.

Me, I 'just wanna have fun' and the next morning I told him so to make it clear.

"I'm enjoying myself too much to think about anything more serious. I've just come out of a relationship that wasn't going anywhere, and I don't want to spend my time locked in another one right now."

Alex nodded, said he understood and that he could

accept things as they were.

"Are you sure about that?" I asked, "Are you sure you can deal with seeing me with other men all the time?"

"Look, Donna," he said, "I've had a great time with you and it's going to get better. As long as you know that I'm the guy who really checks for you, I don't mind being 'friends'."

I wasn't convinced but I left it at that. Men are always saying they want to be friends, but it always end up with them wanting more than that, becoming possessive, and turning up at all times of the night and day and calling round unannounced.

But Alex was right, it had been a great night and it could have gone on that way, if the early morning sun hadn't risen.

"Don't get me wrong," I said, "but I don't really believe in all this fidelity stuff. I believe in love and marriage and everything and I want those things one day, but dating Mr Right, has lost its significance for me. I don't believe that love means that you have to stay with that same person for ever."

Alex insisted that he agreed.

"I don't expect my woman to stay faithful to me forever because I know that just like she needs to take a holiday from work every year, she may need to take a break from me also. As long as she knows that I need to take that break from her as well, everything's cool. I don't think it does any harm, and it probably does some good, because there are people out there whose marriages have been improved by taking a break from each other."

We spent most of the next day together. We started off by having breakfast in bed and staying in bed to read The Observer. He had the broadsheet whilst I read the profiles in the fashion supplement. As it was Sunday we decided to take the underground up to Camden to look around and do some shopping. Alex said that he could see that I loved earrings, and that he would like to surprise me some time with some that he had chosen himself, but he said that he didn't have the confidence to buy them for me, because my taste in them seemed so personal and whacky. I told him to pay closer attention as we browsed through the market stalls and he would see that there was method in my madness.

I first met Lloyd when he came to the restaurant for lunch with a colleague, both carrying an array of mobile phones and beepers. He was only 26, but already owned a string of pirate stations up and down the country. I noticed him straight away and kinda floated across the room towards him to wait on his table. As I took his order, I noticed him undressing me with his eyes. It made me tremble slightly. But he eased my discomfort by making a joke about the lack of spicy food on the menu. He had light eyes and fine, crinkly hair. He continued staring across at me throughout his meal and then blew a kiss across to me as he left. After his generous tip, I felt obliged to return the kiss, giving him the green light to pursue what was on his mind. So that's the way it started.

I agreed to meet up with him on a whim, but had to wait a few weeks for him to clear his other commitments — ducking and diving out of the courts and paying fines for broadcasting illegally. We went for a long drive in his Mercedes 190 on our first date, out of London to Brighton, where we had dinner at an expensive restaurant and then went on to a casino for which he had membership. It was the first time I'd been in a casino and I simply stood by watching the gamblers throwing chips at the croupier and losing them. Somehow Lloyd came out on top and we celebrated with a glass of champagne from the bar, before driving back to London.

On the journey back, with 'dirty soul' filtering softly through the stereo speakers, Lloyd admitted that he had a girlfriend who he was about to dump "because she's a loser, and ignorant" and that he regarded me as 'sex on legs'.

"That's supposed to be a compliment," he added, quickly.

"I like your legs, is that a crime? I'm at a time in my life when I need balance and I think you could give me that balance. When I met you I was like, 'damn, there's something different about this woman' and the way she handles herself."

Lloyd was a much better lover than Alex. He was confident and knew how to handle himself well. He protested that he didn't believe that they made condoms large enough to fit over his manhood. I said, "never mind, stick this over it anyway," and tossed one at him. Compared to Alex, this was mature, adult sex, as dirty as it goes. I had had sex like this before, but I had never met anyone who would interrupt a lovemaking session to answer his phone.

Dating older men wasn't always a good idea. Vernon was 40, and a branch manager of a high street bank. He wasn't exactly handsome, but as far as he was concerned, his main asset was his income. He was old enough to be my father and he handled me gently and tenderly, but he couldn't understand that we weren't suited. He desperately wanted children, but the thought of settling down tied a knot in my stomach! I told him straight — "I ain't the one." On our third date, he produced an engagement ring and said that he loved me. I told him that I loved him too, but I didn't want the ring. It wasn't the first time I had lied to a man, because that was what they wanted to hear. Talk is cheap, and if it makes them happy.

I got the shock of my life when he appeared at the restaurant the next day with several wedding magazines to look through. I spluttered something about everything being rushed through so quickly... and that anyway I was too young to settle down."

He looked dejected but assured me that he wasn't going to give up that easily. He was determined to "make an honest woman" out of me, unless he found someone who better satisfied his needs and was equally attractive, in the meantime.

I tried to laugh the whole thing off, I couldn't believe he was serious, but Vernon didn't see the funny side. He disappeared, embarrassed, and I never heard from him again.

FITNESS

Dee had decided to pick up some provisions at the late night store. She had only just stepped out of her black Audi when she heard a man who was standing outside a spanking new BMW, shout after her: "Baby dat booty bad!"

She turned around angrily, staring at the ebony-skinned man dead in the eyes. He wore a string vest over his t-shirt and dark glasses, and he sported a row of gold teeth, gold 'cargo' hung from his neck, wrists and ears and a mobile phone dangled from his belt.

Dee hadn't learned everything about the British customs and she was still not used to that particular flavour of behaviour that was distinctly Black London.

"Do I know you?" she asked angrily.

The man smiled a bit nervously, hearing her accent.

"So you're a yank?" he asked.

"Look asshole, you wanna talk about somebody's booty, you talk about your mama's, 'cause this is one behind, you just can't touch!"

The man smiled.

"Baby gimme your number man, I like your style."

Dee turned around and walked into the store as the youth called after her.

It was late when Dee got home from work. Carol was sitting in front of the television watching *Imitation Of Life* and her crying her eyes out, whilst caressing a half-empty glass of red wine.

"Hi honey," she said, laying her briefcase down on the

coffee table next to the uncorked wine bottle, "how's your day been?"

"Oh, nothing new," Carol answered looking up from her tissue. "How was yours?"

Dee kicked off her shoes, flopping down on the sofa next to her flat mate and complaining that her job was still demanding more of her time than she had expected.

"I don't know why you watch that film," Dee said, "it always makes you cry."

Carol wiped a tear from her eye and said that was exactly why she always watched it.

"You got a call from your sister, Glenda," Carol informed. "Nothing important, she just wanted to see how you were doing."

"I'm surprised she didn't ask you if I was dating anybody in particular."

"Well actually..."

"You're kidding me!"

"She joked that it will be such a long time before you get hitched up that she will have to accompany you down the aisle in a wheelchair."

Dee frowned.

"That's what I get for coming from a large family of sisters. You know I've organised the weddings of four sisters and been at the birth of 13 nephews and nieces. That's one of the reasons I had to leave Chicago, because all I get is pressure from family and friends to get married. I've been through so many relationships which may have ended in marriage but for whatever reason didn't."

Carol smiled. She understood. Dee was one of a growing number of young and upwardly mobile thirtysomething black women in the dating game and still single who had personally suffered due to the shortage of eligible black men in the professional classes.

"Don't rush it, Dee. You should take all the time you need before deciding to marry. Take a tip from me, that's one thing you don't want to rush through."

Dee assured Carol that despite her single status coming up in all forms of conversation back home, she didn't intend on being pushed into anything.

"I hate it when old friends say something like 'Oh I thought you would be married by now'. Why say that if they know you're single? What purpose does it serve? Everybody wants to know what's wrong with you and how they can help you find a man."

"The one thing they don't tell you," said Carol almost bitterly, "is that if you don't choose carefully, you're better off single."

"As busy as I am," Dee said, "I would gladly make way for a family when the time is right, but to be honest, I think that marrying and having children becomes less likely as time goes by... It makes me sad, but I really believe sometimes that I will never marry... Unless it's to Wesley of course."

Carol laughed. She, Donna and Dee all had a crush on the popular black American actor. They talked about what they would like to do if they got hold of him... They would strap him to a bed all night, or get him in a bubble bath or a sauna or ski down some mountain slope with him, both naked.

"Finding the right person just when the time seems right ain't easy," Dee continued. I've been searching for so long..."

She always selected men who she thought were on the same level as she was intellectually or financially, she explained. Then she started talking freely about the crazy schemes she had come up with over the years to land a suitable partner.

Donna laughed and said that she recognised some of those ideas herself.

"You have to capture a man's attention and then you've got to arouse his interest and then you've got to make him desire you."

"But honey, you know I can sell anything. I sell myself as easily as I sell advertising, by using the most effective methods. But I want the man to sell himself too."

The conversation went like this for a while, before Dee decided to get her bag and go to the gym urging Carol to do the same. Carol agreed.

At the gym, they only had time to for a quick session of squash before closing time, but that was all Dee needed to work off some of the tension that had built up in her after at hard day at the office. When they got home, she sat in a relaxing herbal bath with the light switched off in the bathroom, thinking of nothing and everything for an hour. She had an early start the next morning. Carol also needed the workout at the gym. She felt better for it after the pounds she had recently gained, unable to resist a chocolate chip cookie or two between meals. Carol said that she had nothing special to do the next day except go to the gym with Donna, so she would watch another video before calling it a day.

Upstairs, Dee regarded her face in the bathroom mirror. She had begun to get lines on her forehead. Yet another sign of that biological clock ticking away. She returned to her bedroom and selected an outfit from the wardrobe to wear to work the next day, she considered a nicely knitted navy skirt and jacket, stockings and heeled shoes to be an appropriate outfit for a woman in her position. She remembered the package that had arrived at work for her and pulled it out of her briefcase. It was from Rex Publishing. She opened it to find a collection of Mack Daddy books!

"You know, you're putting on weight," Donna said in her usual frank way.

Carol grimaced. If anything, she didn't need to be reminded that she hadn't been watching what she ate. She was after all *trying* to lose weight.

They were showering in the changing rooms after a strenuous aerobics workout at the gym. As usual the session at the local swimming baths had attracted a number of male onlookers who regularly watched as the fifty or so women went through their routine.

"You gotta keep in shape if you want a man and to regain your confidence, because men only care about how 'fit' a woman is — the size of her breasts, the shape of her hips and if you don't look good, your black man will never be yours entirely, he's gonna look around. And you've got to smile and make them see your dimples... or didn't you know that smiling makes you look more attractive?"

Carol smiled. Donna's concern for her welfare was touching, but she was already getting back on her feet. She had started writing regular film reviews for the local paper which gave her the opportunity to get out and about more and could feel herself becoming more assertive every day.

"You're in such a great shape," she said. She knew that that was one of the reasons Donna always had a myriad of boyfriends, but she was ten years older and it was going to be a long time before she was going to feel good about dating again.

"But," she continued, "it's no good being attractive and getting a lot of a sex but no love."

"Or love and no sex if you're overweight," Donna retorted as quick as a flash.

Yes, she had a point, Carol conceded. "But when you've gone through some painful experiences as I have, you'll know that men figure quite low in the order of things."

"I've been through some painful experiences also, y'know," Donna assured her. "The difference is I don't want to carry it all around with me. I still wanna have some fun in my life, without thinking of all the worthless men out there who I've allowed to diss my life in some way."

Having changed, the two women walked out together, passing through a throng of body-building men, one of whom whistled in their direction.

"You see that," Donna said,"he whistled at you."

Carol smiled. She knew fully well that the man was whistling at Donna.

"You know what I think?" Carol continued. "God should have made men menstruate. If they had a period to deal with every month they would have to cut out all the macho male bullshit and become a lot more sensitive."

Donna laughed.

"You've got to be joking, most of them would top themselves. They couldn't deal with that."

"Even better, men should be the ones who gave birth... They should be the ones who worried about getting pregnant and suffered morning sickness and carried a child for nine months... If men suffered the pain of child birth, they wouldn't carry on their lives having casual relationships here and there and everywhere. They'd have to think carefully before having their end away.

Donna laughed even louder.

"That wouldn't stop them... They love sex too much. No amount of pain is going to stop them getting it."

Carol thought for a moment and agreed. It was improbable to think that any amount of inconvenience would stop men in their pursuit for sex.

"All they want out of a relationship is good looks and sex but they make out like they want the same things as women do like charm, maturity, honesty, warmth. Have you ever met a man who really wanted all those things instead of sex and good looks?"

Donna had to admit that despite her wide experience of men, she hadn't.

"You see what I mean?" Carol continued. "Right up to the day he died, my grandfather used to bring my grandmother breakfast in bed everyday and he would always lay a fresh rose on the tray. When I asked him why he did this, he said, he wanted to make sure that whatever happened during the day, she would know that he woke up that morning in love with her."

"Mmmn... isn't that a wicked story," Donna said dreamily, "your grandfather sounds like the kind of man I've been looking for all my life."

It was the type of man that most women wanted, Carol added, but she hadn't met any man that treated his woman as well as grandad did. For most men romance was about having a huge dick and fucking like crazy...

Donna listened as Carol drifted off in her own thoughts. A sadness in her housemate's voice revealed the real life sorrow in Carol's heart.

"So your husband, Neville, he's still crawling about somewhere under your skin, isn't he?" Donna asked.

"Neville? No, I'm over him..."

Donna looked at her friend sceptically.

"Look, I wouldn't give him the cake of mud off the

bottom of my shoe," Carol insisted. "It's just that my whole marriage would have been pointless if I haven't learned anything from it. Maybe I do want to find another man, but right now I don't want to be out there looking for a man and ending up with someone who is just like Neville."

"Maybe you shouldn't have any high expectations and just do like I do and date for fun. Me, I can let a man think that I am really crazy over him, but I'm actually just in there to get what I want from it and then 'see you later' and every now and then I make a man scream all night with pleasure, just because I'm having such a good time myself."

Donna and Carol had a good laugh about that one on the rest of the short walk home.

LET'S TALK ABOUT SEX

The postcard from Andre was waiting for me at the office when I arrived for work the morning after I moved in with Carol and Donna. It was the first personal contact either of us had made since our evening together at the hotel in New York. I read it with a smile as I was once again reminded of the man my heart and mind had told me was the man I had been looking for:

Hello Homegirl,
You're on my mind at the strangest of times. Wish we could have had more evenings together.
If you're in Chicago, give me a call.
Lots of Love
Andre.

I glanced at the photo on the front, a scene from the movie *When Harry Met Sally*. I read Andre's words again unsure of their meaning. He hadn't mentioned his fiancee, which left me hanging confused. I resolved to drop him a card with my new address.

The deal at work was this: Julian was paid off and laid off and I was promoted to the then vacant post of account executive — with a higher salary and a company car, the company would never hear anything about a law suit for sexual harassment. That sounded fine to me. I managed to keep Helen as my secretary also and got them to throw in a salary raise for her at the same time. After all, it was she who had suggested the tape recorder trap, when I had told her about Julian's real motives.

In many ways, my new job was less demanding than being creative director. The only problem was that as account executive I had to lead the team and inspire them. I was used to working with a bunch of white guys either on the same level as them or as their superior so that part was nothing new. I wasn't prepared however, to have to work with a bunch of advertising guys who really didn't want to sell anything. What is it about the British that they are so embarrassed about selling themselves? Splash's creative minds spent their time dreaming up witty and clever TV and radio commercials but found the hard sell 'distasteful'. The agency had managed to hang on to its existing clients only because it was more convenient than going elsewhere. But that wouldn't last forever if their products weren't selling. Clients weren't interested in how many awards the agency had won, they wanted to sell. It was time the agency decided if it wanted to sell the product or make a clever ad. In the States, the three rules of advertising are sell, sell and sell: "You gotta a headache? Try this, it will make you feel better. You haven't got a headache? Try this, it will make you feel better."

Basically, the public weren't going out and buying the products that Splash worked on. The PR company of one of our clients was even upset because they felt that the advertising campaign hadn't featured their client in a good light and they had sent a letter indicating that the client was now 'reviewing' all of its existent advertising commitments, which meant that we were being fired as an ad agency. That was serious. I had to get tough. I called a meeting for the whole department, to announce the start of a new campaign.

They were all in the boardroom on time, the creatives,

the media planners, media buyers, photographers, artists and illustrators.

"The first thing I want to say is that you all know me by now and you all know my name is Dee... I've heard all the jokes about dee-*cease*, dee-*feet*, dee-*lay*, dee-*kay*, dee-*light*, dee-*liver*, dee-*note* and dee-*va*. Unless anyone objects, I'd like you to finish enjoying the joke today, so that we can start working from tomorrow..."

I looked around the room at each person one by one. There was no descent. I had made up my mind to kick butt.

"Next, the business we are in is advertising," I spelt it out in big and bold capital letters on the board behind me. "Translated, it means the business of selling something that no one wants, to people who can't afford it."

I looked slowly around the room. The faces in front of me had quizzical expressions. I hadn't expected them to appreciate it, but it was at times like this that I was grateful for what I remembered of my Master's degree in Communication.

"Consumers don't always know why they buy a product," I continued my argument, "that's why we all get paid nice fat salaries, to tell them what they want."

It was time to deal with the individual jobs. I started with the planners and worked my way up.

"So how come this production is going to cost much more than the client said he could afford?"

The planners are the people who research the product to start off with — what kind of people will buy it, *why* they will want to buy it and what socio-economic group they belong to. Planners are usually comprised of new university graduates desperate to get into advertising and feeling that they can do everybody else's job better than them. They also decide which magazines are suitable to purchase advertising for the product. I didn't care how many intelligent people the agency had, who spent hours thinking big flash clever thoughts and shots. The clients needed to know what they were getting what they wanted, which was increasing sales, and I had to explain how it would be done.

One of the graduates shuffled about in her seat uneasily before speaking.

"We ran into unexpected costs, the product had to be fully researched to make sure there was a market for it. And then we decided that if the client spent more money on the campaign we could do a thorough job. I'm sure people in Manchester would go for it also, but the budget was initially for London alone...With all due respect Dee, every client says they can't afford a penny more but when push comes to shove they usually can."

"That's not the point," I fired back. "The client pays your salary, he calls the shots. From now on any increase in budget comes directly out of your salaries."

Somewhere amongst them I heard somebody curse quietly, but I let it go. I had more fish to fry.

"And another thing," I added, "stop producing reams and reams of paperwork; it's impossible to go through all those figures and statistics anyway. What I want to know from the planning department is whether people like the product or not, and which people liked the product and which people didn't."

Every copywriter is a failed poet and as such are very sensitive. But that didn't trouble me, I was on the warpath — determined to initiate U.S. business methods to the traditional English work practices. It was the copywriter's job to write the words used on an ad or spoken on a radio or TV commercial. Everybody thinks they can do the job, but to do it well ain't that easy. I decided that it was about time that someone knocked the egos of these 'writers-in-residence'

"Maybe you should consider getting a job on a poetry magazine," I chastised the one copywriter who spent his days dreaming up fancy captions that couldn't sell anything. He blushed a deep red and avoided my gaze, probably thinking, 'who the hell does this yank think she is?' They hadn't come to terms with having a woman superior, let alone a black woman. Well that was too bad, I intended to make sure they knew who was boss and what I expected from them, before the meeting came to a close.

I pulled out a couple of books on copywriting from my briefcase and threw them across the polished table at the copywriters.

"Read them," I ordered, "if you can't come up with a good original idea, plagiarise one of the examples of great advertising featured in these books. If it was a good ad before it's still good now, people haven't changed that much... Revamp the idea and make it something new for the nineties."

I looked around the room once more at each anxious face — as it dawned on them that this was a totally new regime — and wondered why it was necessary to have so many people working on an account. I made a mental note to let some of them go, because it didn't follow that the more staff employed the better the campaign would be. It was more important to expand the marketing department, whilst instilling the remaining employees with a new vigour and thoroughness.

I turned to the art director — who was staring moodily into space as he had been doing the whole meeting. He had an expensive habit of calling in freelancers when he was stuck for an idea. As the art director, he should never be stuck for an idea. That's what he was getting paid for. I had already decided his fate, so I left him for the meanwhile.

The meeting came to an end finally, with me asking for suggestions for the new project by the next day.

Every night for the next two weeks, I lay in bed thinking about Andre; wondering what he was doing and if he was doing it with his woman; if he was... Lucky her! I wondered if he thought about me as much as I thought about him and whether I could will him to give me a call. Could I really go for a man who I hardly knew this much? Maybe it was something to do with the fact that I was away from home in a foreign country and suddenly able to see everything in the perspective of the tick tock of the biological clock inside me, reminding me that I was thirty years old and still single. Now it was my turn to start brooding and questioning what I was doing with my life. I started longing to be back home in the States, if only to get the opportunity to convince Andre that I was the perfect woman for him.

I couldn't believe what I was doing, but here I was driving back to Wimbledon in my Audi, with a handsome young man at my side and kissing and cuddling every time I stopped at a traffic light. I hadn't even intended to go to the brasserie in Brixton after work, but it was Friday evening and nothing special was happening and suddenly I was there, relaxing with a drink in front of me and watching the lively 'thank God it's Friday' early evening crowd coming in.

Maybe I was really hoping to meet someone, but I was still surprised when a handsome, young hunk of a man with a charming smile and a polite nature about him came up to where I was sitting by myself and asked if he could buy me a drink. I looked up at him and smiled.

"No thanks," I said, pointing to an almost full glass of beer, but wishing I had said 'yes'.

"Well at least allow me to bring my drink over here and join you."

I'm not in the habit of picking men up in bars or being picked up in bars. But the invitation was innocent enough, so I told him to go ahead. The seat was vacant anyway. He went to fetch his drink and sat down opposite me. He introduced himself as Harvey and explained that he had just popped into the brasserie for a drink and was considering going on to a party in North London afterwards. He was a part-time model and a full-time student at East Herts University reading mathematics. He explained that he wasn't stupid enough to rely on his looks for success like so many other male models.

"With female models you find quite a few who are really clever business women, but male models have got a bad reputation of not having anything between their ears," he said regretfully, "and when you meet most guys in the business, you understand why. My rule of thumb when I meet another male model is that the handsomer they are the more stupid they are."

Harvey looked older, but when I found out he was only 23 years I laughed and said that I was old enough to be his lecturer. He looked at me straight in the eye, holding his gaze for a moment.

"I think I would like that very much," he said firmly.

I thought about it for a second, but decided it was best to let it drop. We continued talking. He seemed very interested in what I was doing and he seemed to know a lot about the advertising industry.

"Well, if you're ever looking for a black model for one of your campaigns, maybe you could give me a call. I could always do with some more work, it helps me pay for my studies, you know."

He said that it made a change meeting a black American woman in London, because there were so few and that he had always wanted to visit the States. He had a sister in Philadelphia who was always inviting him over, but he had never made it across, to see her.

"That's what I love about modelling the best," he said, "despite all the long hours and hard work, it gives you a chance to travel. The places I've been to, I'm telling you, one moment in Paris, the next in Milan, and I've even been to Tokyo one time for a magazine fashion shoot. I could never have afforded to go to so many places without the job."

I don't know exactly when the point came in the evening that I decided that I was going to go home with Harvey that night. Though neither of us said anything, 'sex' was in the air. Harvey said that he shared a tiny room in Clapham with a friend, which left me no choice but to invite him home to Wimbledon. Shortly after we left the brasserie I started thinking that maybe things weren't going to be all that bad for me in London after all.

It was already late when we arrived back in Wimbledon. The lights were all out and I supposed that Carol had gone to bed and that Donna was out as she usually was on a Friday evening.

I turned the key in the front door and led the way in. Suddenly the reality of what I was doing hit home to me as I stood in the familiar surroundings of the living room. I was bringing home a man for the first time in my new London home, a man who I had only just met. It was crazy. Whenever girlfriends in Chicago had confided that they had picked up men in bars and gone home with them, wasn't it always *me* who told them *they* were crazy, and here I was doing exactly the same thing. Somehow, I felt totally safe however. It was hard for me to imagine a man with a British accent as anything but a gentleman.

"Maybe this isn't a good idea," I said, hoping he would confirm that.

"Anything you say," Harvey replied. "I'll stay for just one cup of coffee, then I'll phone for a cab," he said, reassuringly.

I thought about how many times I had heard a man say that and how many times it hadn't turned out that way. I should have shown him the door immediately if I was serious about it being a bad idea, but I couldn't suddenly decide to send him on his way after driving him so far out of his way. At the same time it wasn't like I had anything against his company. Harvey had managed to chase away my blues and cheer me up when I was low. I thought for a moment about Andre's postcard and wished that Harvey was the Chicago police Lieutenant who I really wanted in my life. But Andre had Shawna, his fiancee, I had nobody and I was longing for some intimacy in my life.

Harvey made himself comfortable in the living room flicking through the magazines on the coffee table, issues of Premiere, Newsweek, Essence and Marie Claire.

"Oh so you read Pride magazine regularly?" I joked when I returned with the coffees.

"I just like looking at the photos in women's magazines."

"Pride is the best black woman's magazine I've seen," I said. "The States has got Essence magazine, and that's good, but I couldn't believe there was a magazine for me

104

in the UK which was even better."

Harvey wasted no time in drinking his coffee, then waited patiently for me to swallow the remaining contents of my cup before putting his arm around my shoulders and gently massaging my back for me. For a man of 23, he knew what he was doing and he gently probed all my tense spots, relaxing me. It wasn't long before we were kissing passionately on the sofa. I knew then that my resistance was broken and that Harvey wouldn't be calling a cab home that night.

Before I knew it I was sitting astride his lap with my skirt hitched up to my waist and his zip pulled down. I was glad he was sensible and had taken a condom from his pocket. My whole body seemed to explode as he entered me, slowly and stiffly. It seemed to go on for ever, before he was fully in, deep inside me. I felt excited and confused as I moved slowly up and down on him, only just managing to catch myself from exhaling a loud and long-awaited sigh of pleasure. It was nerve-racking. Suppose Carol heard a noise and came down? I put my fingers up to my lips as Harvey's breathing became heavier and louder until he was almost gasping for breath. We had to be extremely quiet. I continued cautiously but firmly, raising my hips up higher and letting them down harder and faster each time. I ran my fingers through my hair, enjoying every minute of it. I wanted to thank Harvey, because it felt so good. But there were more ways to love a black woman, and I wanted to roll around with him on my mattress, unrestrained and without anxiety. I coaxed Harvey upstairs. He was so powerful he lifted me up, still inside me with my legs knotted tightly around his waist and carried me up the stairs effortlessly, his muscles bulging under his shirt as he did so. I ran a finger across them and felt the tensed-up power. I was in heaven and I didn't want it to end. We went as softly as possible along the upstairs corridor. But I forgot about the loose floorboard outside Carol's room which seemed to shatter the silence in the house.

"Who's that!" my house mate's voice called from her bedroom.

"Oh Carol, it's only me," I called back, catching my breath for a moment. "Don't get up, I'm going to bed. See you in the morning. Good night."

Harvey carried me the rest of the short way to my room and still locked together, we continued to make beautiful love on the bed.

The sun streaming through the window woke me up the next morning. I looked at the clock. It was already midday. It was Saturday so it didn't matter that I had overslept. Then I remembered the night before. Harvey it seemed had already got up and gone. He was nowhere around and neither were his clothes, nor my pocket book or my car keys. I rushed to the window and looked out onto the road in front. My car was gone!

WAKE UP AND LIVE

The stereo in the living room was turned up to full volume. It was the middle of the day and Carol was alone in the house dancing and singing *I Will Survive* along with Gloria Gaynor.

Everything was turning out fine. She had just been accepted to Law School in the autumn to pursue the career she should have followed after her degree, she had two great girl friends as flatmates and she had succeeded in banishing Neville from her thoughts. It was his loss. She knew what she was worth and she would never again settle for less. If she was interested, there were lots of men out there who were a lot more giving than Neville. And if she could only find another bastard, she'd make sure at least that he was a lot handsomer next time.

It was like being given a new lease of life. And she was taking care of herself a lot better also, with a strict 'no crisps' rule in her house and by following a regular fitness and aerobics programme down at the gym. She had even got rid of the wide screen colour television in her bedroom, which had comforted her with romantic late night movies during her difficult time. The next door neighbours' kids were delighted when the lady-next-door presented them with the TV.

Carol hadn't felt this good in years, fresh and 'born again'. She intended to have fun in the next few months before becoming a student again and she was determined not to allow any man to mess up her vibes.

She had made herself feel good for herself, likewise

she aimed to make herself look good, for herself. She splashed out on miracle anti-ageing creams and beautiful clothes, she went and got her hair done once a week and started using make-up again. And as she got fitter, she threw out everything in her wardrobe and bought a whole new set of what she considered to be classy clothing but which Donna described as 'dry'. She even got her teeth straightened as she had wanted to for so long. It made a big dent in her meagre savings, but she would have borrowed money if necessary, it was worth every penny. And if that didn't help with her self-confidence, she had the American self-improvement cassette tapes with positive information Dee had lent her – *Learn To Love Yourself* and *Success In A Month? Ask Me How.*

If she could feel good and better by herself she could get on with her life without having to consider any man.

And she read voraciously during this time, books on African fiction, travel books and her favourite romance fiction.

"Yeah," she said aloud as Gloria's vocals faded out, "I'm a survivor."

Carol's sister Janice started coming around more regularly when she learned of the break-up of her sister's marriage, to encourage her to think positive.

"You're only 34," she said, "you're just a spring chicken with the whole of your life ahead of you."

Janice was 28 and had been happily married for eleven years to Ollie. They had two kids, Shannon, 10 and Martin 7, and had managed to stay together despite their differences. Ollie was the old-fashioned type who believed in the husband being the breadwinner and he was always complaining that he earned enough money for the both of them so Janice didn't need to work. Janice however, was staunchly independent and Ollie had known this back in their schooldays when they first met. She loved nursing too much to quit and still harboured dreams of one day becoming a doctor.

Recently Janice had begun to invite herself around to her sister's in the company of Ollie's unattached friends.

"Oh me and Greg were just passing by, so I suggested we drop in for a cuppa," Janice said with a wink to her sister.

Carol didn't mind her sister dropping by any time she wanted to, but as she had already explained several times, she had better things to do with her time than "run after man all day long." Janice seemed determined not to heed her sister's request not to be 'fixed up'. Fortunately Carol succeeded in frightening most of them away.

Greg, was 35 and like Ollie, a powerfully-built fireman. The first thing Carol asked him when Janice brought him over, was why he wasn't home looking after his kids, then she made the tea.

He assured her confidently that he didn't have any kids.

"You mean you don't have any kids anywhere?" she asked as they sat around the coffee table in the conservatory.

"Nope."

Carol could see Janice staring at her intensely, indicating that she should change the subject, but she ignored her.

"Are you sure there isn't a Greg junior somewhere who you've forgotten about?"

"Definitely not. It's hardly something I'm going to forget about."

"So what's wrong with you then?" Carol said sharply,

"medical problem, is it?"

"Nothing like that... I guess I just haven't found the right woman."

"Well, you better keep looking, hadn't you," Carol advised. "I mean you're not getting any younger are you?"

Greg looked at Janice helplessly, with an expression that said 'what did I do wrong'?

Janice shrugged her shoulders and fired an icy stare in her sister's direction. For a moment Carol wondered if she had gone too far. But it was too late to begin regarding Greg as a potential date.

"Look, the only reason I came up here was because of Janice. I was doing her a favour," the fireman said coldly, getting up to leave. "She said you were desperate, I can see why..."

Greg didn't even bother to thank his hostess for the tea.

Janice turned briefly to her sister, shaking her head, before following the fireman out.

"I didn't say 'desperate'," she called out with a warning finger, "I said 'available'."

Janice didn't give up, when it came to finding unattached men, she seemed to have unlimited resources and the unshaken belief that there was a good man out there for her sister, all she had to do was find him.

Victor was the next guy who happened to call, because Janice had given him her sister's number. He was a 38-year-old stand-up comic with a sense of humour that could come in useful. He had obviously been briefed on how difficult Carol was going to be, because he replied to her lack of enthusiasm over the phone, by sending twelve yellow roses around the next day and then passing by later that evening to check that they had arrived.

With the fragrance of fresh flowers and a reassuring smile he stood on her doorstep.

"Hi, you must be Carol," Victor said, taking off his hat to Dee.

Dee looked him up and down. He was dressed immaculately and seemed impeccably groomed and he had a wide smile to go with what essentially looked like a happy face.

"Hold on," the American woman replied and went in to let her flat mate know that "a cute brother" was standing on the door step with another bunch of yellow roses.

Carol sighed when Victor introduced himself at the door.

"I thought I told you not to bother coming around?" she said, maintaining her stony 'Black Man Done Me Wrong' look.

"I'm not here to distress you," Victor joked, raising his hand, "I just forgot to send these along with the delivery this morning," he said, presenting Carol with another dozen roses.

She took them reluctantly, thinking that he had overdone the flowers slightly. She didn't mind being surprised with a rose once in a while, but gifts didn't impress her; anything she needed she could get herself.

"So won't you ask me in?"

Carol studied him for a moment. It wasn't that she had anything against inviting him in, it was just that her Donna and Dee were at home arguing about Donna's overuse of the telephone and Dee not returning Donna's hairdryer and she didn't want this man embarrassing her with any corny lines in front of her friends.

"Well, I'm just on my way out," she lied.

"Well, let me accompany you."

"Suit yourself," Carol said, and she went inside briefly for a jacket, before stepping out into the early evening.

She kept up a steady pace, walking down the road, with Victor keeping up as best he could at her side.

He said he preferred to walk hand-in-hand with women, which sounded really stupid to Carol, so she ignored him and continued walking. She didn't know where she was going, just going for a walk, anywhere until Victor had had enough.

"You see, I'm a bit of a romantic..." he said, panting slightly to keep up. "And as I'm sure you know, being a romantic is very unusual for a real black man."

"Who says so?" Carol asked unimpressed. "Did you read it somewhere? Did your father tell you that? Did you see it in a film?"

"No, nothing like that," Victor protested, "I just thought that that was common knowledge."

They had barely gone far when he came out suddenly and announced that he was unattached.

"Why are you telling me that?" Carol asked almost angrily.

"I was just letting you know for future reference," Victor said sheepishly. "Bwoy," he said slapping himself on the forehead, "Yuh is hard work, yah know dat. I can't understand it... I always seem to chase women away..."

Carol took pity on him briefly. She stopped walking and paused long enough to explain:

"Look, it's not you, there's nothing wrong with you, you're fine, it's me. I'm just not interested."

She turned and walked backwards to the house, leaving the comedian standing by himself on the pavement.

But Victor didn't give up that easy. The next day her answering machine was filled with Victor performing a live rendition of *Oh Carolina.*

Donna and Dee were already clapping in time to the message when she arrived. Fortunately, Carol saw the funny side of things. Her friends both thought that it was a romantic gesture which Carol should respond to positively. But she wasn't ready. She hadn't been asked out in a long time and now she was inundated with offers but preferred to wait for the right time and the right man with the right attitude.

It took another week before Victor gave up entirely, after sending her a different parcel every day. First it was a box of matches, the next day it was a wall thermometer, then a bottle of tabasco sauce, then a parcel containing a kilo of chilli peppers. Finally he sent a postcard of a lazy beach in the Caribbean on which he had written the message, "I've got the hots for you." However much Victor huffed and puffed, he wasn't able to blow this woman's mind.

Carol would have relented and put him out of his misery if this was any other time, but her marriage break-up had hardened her heart.

Janice suspected as much when she came by to visit after Victor had given up.

"Are you sure you've managed to come to terms with life after Neville?" she asked Carol. "And that you've put him far enough behind you? Because you don't want to keep that bad attitude with you. You gotta change that attitude because you're scaring all the men away."

Carol assured her sister that Neville was history, but that she was older and wiser and she just didn't have the time to make mistakes as she had made earlier.

"I don't need a man," she insisted again, making light of her romantic 'failures', "not unless he's nineteen years old, wears corduroy trousers, has at least one broken

marriage behind him and speaks with a French accent...
Look, I just enjoy being single, I don't want a lifelong
partner and I don't need a part-time man."

Janice ignored her sister's levity. Carol was still on
'married woman' mode and found it difficult to 'switch
over' to single status.

"I know what your problem is, you don't want to sell
yourself too short, you want to make a good 'catch' first
time."

Janice said she had the perfect answer. Dalton Browne.
He was just the kind of man Carol would be attracted to:
imaginative, insightful, communicative, affectionate,
harmonious and supportive, with "very good potential."

Carol sighed.

"You don't know when to give up do you?"
Janice said she would give up if her sister at least gave
this guy a chance.

Carol thought about it for a moment.

"Okay, but this is definitely the last man you fix up for
me."

"Sure, sure. Don't worry about that."

And he's only getting one chance to make an
impression. No second date."

"He won't need one. You'll see," she said smiling,
"you'll like him, as long as you're not expecting Einstein,
he won't expect you to be Naomi Campbell. And this
time, I'll set everything up."

Janice called the next day, she had spoken to Dalton
who was agreeable and free any evening. Carol agreed on
a day and time. A few days later she received a formal
invitation from Janice 'requesting the pleasure of her
company' with the day, time and address. 'Dress strictly
formal'.

Had Carol met Dalton anywhere else, she may have

treated him to the same disdain as her earlier suitors. But she had never been on a river boat restaurant before and she was looking forward to the experience. They met on the embankment at 7.30 sharp. Dalton was already there to receive her as she stepped out of a black cab on the Embankment, dressed in an elegant black woollen two-piece. He looked impressive with Dax-oiled hair slicked back and shiny, an immaculate dinner suit with dress shirt and well-shined black shoes.

However well he hid it, Carol could always tell when a man fancied her. She could read it in his eyes. She caught Dalton stealing surreptitious glances at her bosom and behind on more than one occasion as they climbed onto the deck of The Caribbean Queen.

The boat moved off on its cruise Eastwards down the Thames. They sat down on the restaurant deck amongst the other diners as the lights of the city drifted by on the shore. A lone pianist tinkled away at one end, filling the atmosphere inside with some unobtrusive dinner jazz.

"You know what my fantasy is?" Dalton began, "It's to leave the rat race and get a little sailing boat and to sail over to the Caribbean and just go island-hopping for a few years, with my only worry being where to go next — Port of Spain, Georgetown or Negril."

"So you're a dreamer?" Carol asked, unable to resist a little irony.

Dalton Browne, was 37 and a partner at a firm of chartered accountants in the city. A tall, well-built Jamaican, he could have passed for a black James Bond and carried himself like someone of means. He was a single woman's dream and he also owned two homes and an expensive car. For all his worth he could have been a pauper as far as Carol was concerned. She was having an evening out and that was all that mattered. A uniformed waiter took their orders. Carol went for the fish, with a side dish of salad. Dalton ordered the chicken, no salad. The conversation was cordial throughout and touched on the situation in Haiti with America declaring itself 'the world's police', and the latest theatre openings int he West End. Carol was on her best behaviour, giving her companion an opportunity to prove his bright, easy-going, open and sensitive credentials.

"Don't you dream?" Dalton asked when the food arrived.

"Not really," Carol quick-fired back. "Not any more."

"Pity," Dalton said."Dreams kept me alive when my wife left me."

Dalton explained that he was on the rebound from a relationship.

"It took me a long time to trust women again, after the way my ex-woman handled me," he continued, slowly and deliberately. "I don't understand how she could have been cheating for so long. She told me she was attending evening classes..."

What cut him up, he explained was not just that his woman had been unfaithful, but that when she told him about it, she already had all her bags packed and was ready to move in with her lover. He hadn't suspected anything because she was his woman, why should he suspect anything? If she wasn't happy why didn't she talk to him about it?

"You've got to trust your partner haven't you, as much as your partner's got to trust you."

"Were you ever unfaithful during the relationship?"

"Never," Dalton insisted.

The conversation had touched so close to her own situation that it made Carol uncomfortable. Neville was the last thing she wanted to think about while drifting down the Thames feasting on salmon and champagne.

"Usually it's the men who think nothing of lying and being dishonest," Carol said finally, unsympathetically. Isn't that all part of the game that you've been playing in relationships since the beginning of time?"

" 'You' who? I haven't. There are some black men out there who respect their women too much to behave that way."

"So how comes you haven't found anybody since?" Carol asked, changing the subject.

"I'm more careful now. I can't afford to make a mistake the next time around. I still want to build a family and share my life with someone special. I want someone I can really devote myself to, but I'm too old to be disappointed again."

Carol smiled. It was sweet that Dalton, despite his marital experiences still believed that one could fall in love and live happily ever after and still valued the traditional elements of love such as fidelity. Dreaming, Carol concluded, was not for her:

"If only it was that simple..." she said half to herself. "I thought accountants were supposed to be very reasoned people. Is there really such a thing as a romantic accountant?"

"Why, shouldn't there be?"

Carol didn't reply.

"Something's troubling you?" Dalton said as they walked and talked on deck after dinner, a gentle spring breeze following them on their way back up the Thames to town.

"Oh you know, I've had my own problems recently," Carol said, her head light with champagne and becoming momentarily sentimental.

"Won't you tell me about your problems, maybe I can

help you solve them."

She could have told him so much. She could have said that she was a casualty of love, worn and battered and no longer willing to experience the low moments of a relationship just in order to experience the occasional 'highs'. She wanted to weed out the 'no hopers' from her life and find someone who could fulfil her emotional needs if there was such a man out there. Carol could have told Dalton all these things, but she chose not to.

"Let's just enjoy this beautiful night," she said, leaning her head back over the safety rail. "Let's not spoil it."

Carol was right, the night was like magic and they were still staring up at the sky when the boat pulled into its mooring at the Embankment.

Back on the street, Dalton flagged down a black taxi and they climbed in the back. Carol said that he didn't have to follow all the way to Wimbledon, but he insisted.

"I wouldn't dream of abandoning you at this point," he said.

"I won't even be able to invite you in for a cup of coffee, because my flat mates will be in bed..."

"I'm not doing this so that I can be invited in for coffee."

The taxi came to a halt by the Houses of Parliament, where it waited for a red light.

Dalton was talking, about how many children he some day hoped to have. For some reason, Carol felt a set of eyes upon her. She looked out of the window on Dalton's side, where Neville's blue Mazda sports car was also waiting at the light. He was staring right into the back of the cab, straight at her. Almost without thinking, Carol slipped her arm around Dalton's waist and pulled him towards her, engaging in a long, passionate kiss. He was surprised at her sudden upbeat attitude, but delighted also and he made sure that his embrace was warm and considerate. Carol found herself enjoying it; it had been so long since she had been so close to a man.

RAGGA TO RICHES

The make up man said he had never seen a face like mine, so perfectly shaped and skin so unblemished. It would be a pleasure to work on my face, he said. He mixed the colours expertly on the back of his hand with a soft brush and set about making me look sexy.

It was my first video shoot, I was on my way to achieving what I came to London to do. The make-up man worked on silently, barely making a sound. I stared into the mirror and waited. My stomach was full of butterflies as my face slowly took on a new beauty I had never seen before. I felt like a star and looked forward to the time when I would consider this experience commonplace.

Dance hall fashion doesn't pretend to be 'fashion'. It's more like 'bare as you dare' — anything you feel comfortable with. Clothes which other people call tacky or slack, are *haute couture* in the dancehall. Sequins, see through clothing, fishnet stockings and extra tight leather shorts are definitely in, baggy clothes definitely out. Church people are always describing dancehall queens as coarse, crude and rough, but check how the thing's turned, because nowadays everyone wants to book dance hall 'models' for shows, thanks to Shabba's videos.

If you're gonna get noticed, you need to dare to bare more than anyone else. That's why I dress more extravagantly than anyone else and dance more outrageously. That's why men are always describing me as 'sexy', despite my having thighs some people would call 'chubby' and a big bum. But I'm proud of my body and men like it that way.

I was wearing my favourite peroxide blonde wig and green contact lenses, with a tight dress and panty hose, dancing in the middle of the dancehall at the Bass Academy — one of the successful new clubs that had sprung up in south London — when I was spotted by Colin, who was tall and skinny with round wire glasses.

"Are you a model by any chance?" he shouted in my ear above the boom of the music.

I looked at him suspiciously before answering. I had heard so many different chat up lines that I was weary of the slightest move. But this guy was different. I nodded my head and he handed me his card, which stated that he was a photographer.

"I'm doing a video for Reggie Fury. I want you to be in it. Give me a call."

I nodded and said I would. Reggie was one of my favourite artists, a sexy soul singer with a reputation for being able to hit a woman in her 'G Spot' and make her moan, "oooh" and "aaah". I had already seen one of his videos and knew that they had a reputation for being steamy and not for those with a delicate disposition.

The video was being shot at a huge warehouse in West London. Colin had asked me to come in my most outrageous outfit. This show was too important to too many people to allow hitches such as the wrong clothes being worn. I dressed in a bright orange leather batty rider over fishnet stockings and a low-cut matching top, short enough to leave my midriff bare. I wore a diamond stud through my nose, oversize earrings in my ears and a ruby in my belly button. Again I wore a peroxide blonde wig, but this time, cut short to a bob, as well as a spare selection of the latest outfits wrapped in a protective plastic. It was a very long day. Me and the six other models danced seductively for hours as Reggie lay on a bed with satin sheets wearing nothing but a G-string and miming to his latest tune, *XTC*. When everything was through and the models were preparing to leave, Colin suddenly came over to me and asked me to stay behind so that he could try out some alternative shots with just me and Reggie.

As I turned to join Reggie on the bed again, I heard the cameraman whisper, "she's got the best tits in the video, her figure is unbeatable."

The other models hung about looking on as I snogged away with Reggie on the bed for the re-shoot. It was hard to see what they were thinking, but they must have been pissed off at all the attention I was being given.

The cameraman circled around the set, trying to get perfect angles for every shot and made us do it over and over again until he was satisfied.

Reggie drove me home in his Suzuki Vitara jeep after the shoot was finally over. He also looked great with his clothes on, wearing designer everything, including boxer shorts with his name across the waistband, clearly visible above his baggy black denims.

"Tell me," Reggie said, peering over his Ray-Bans at me as he handled the steering like an expert through the near-deserted streets, heading south, "do a lot of men lust after you?"

I asked him what kind of question that was to ask a lady and he replied that he didn't mean any offense and that it was just that I had turned him on all the way through the video shoot.

Reggie looked at me hard. He turned down the volume on the stereo, until the music from the swingbeat tape merely rocked gently.

"You see, I have a lot of women lusting after me. Pure lust and everything they want to do with me has something to do with sex."

"I'm not surprised," I said letting out a giggle, "after all, you are the 'G-spot' man, aren't you?"

He smiled.

"I hate to admit it, but being able to get any woman I want to is ruining the loving and caring side of my nature."

"I personally don't mind if a man lusts after me," I assured him, "but some of my girlfriends might feel offended if a man came on to them that strongly. Man shall not live by lust alone!"

I tend to be more interested in sex than most of the men I meet. Long after they think the job's done, I'm still craving for more, teasing and taunting them until they give me what I want. Sex for me was always hot and heavy.

"Do you have problems having sex very early on in a relationship?"

I turned to Reggie and studied him for a moment, trying to decide wither I fancied him or merely lusted after him. All these questions seemed to be leading to the inevitable, but as yet he kept his cards close to his chest. A lot of people have to shop around for that one relationship which is exciting and special, someone who is unlike everybody else they've ever met. But Reggie seemed to have fallen out of the sky onto my lap.

Okay, he wasn't a genius, but who wants to sleep with an Einstein? But he was Reggie Fury and a successful pop star and sex symbol. Which woman would turn him down? Every time I thought about the fact that I was actually been driven home by him in his jeep, it blew my mind. I couldn't just let him slip away. I'm the type of woman who when I see a man I fancy, just walks up to him and chats him up. But this was Reggie's show, he had to make the move so that I could find out exactly what he was after.

No, I replied, sex early in a relationship didn't bother me.

He didn't add anything to that, but kept his eyes on the road and kept driving, scratching his goatee every now and then, as if he was considering different propositions.

We eventually arrived outside my place in Wimbledon and Reggie parked up on the pavement right in front of the gate. He quickly jumped out and went around to my side to let me out. He still hadn't made his move.

"Are you sure you won't be too lonely by yourself upstairs?" he asked as we said our goodbyes.

"I'm used to it, why are you offering to keep me company?"

He said that it was just a suggestion. I looked at him and smiled.

"Come on in," I said.

SKINTEETH

Carol shook her head again. She was too old for the outfit. If she was ten years younger maybe, but it was too revealing, the colours too bright.

"It's not exactly me," she protested.

"That's just the point," Donna continued. "We came here to find something which wasn't you, remember?"

Carol frowned. Donna was right. She wasn't herself anyway. She was no longer a married woman and she had to start thinking like a single woman again. And if she wanted to halt the rut of television and popcorn she had ground herself into and start going out instead, she would need some party clothes. But maybe she should have gone shopping for clothes with Dee instead. They were closer in age and had near enough the same tastes.

"It's a bit too flash. You try it, Donna."

Donna sighed. They had been traipsing around Finsbury Park all morning. Like so many other fashion conscious black women, she frequented the Greek and Turkish owned wholesalers on Fonthill Road to not only purchase the latest styles, but to get them at manufacturer's prices. They had been to a dozen different stores already and Carol had still not been sold on anything she had seen.

"I'm telling you Carol, this dress will suit you perfectly. You can go to any dance or party with this and have men's heads spinning."

"Maybe I need a dress which will get a couple of guys to turn their heads. Maybe something a bit looser."

"But what did you lose all that weight for? What was all that aerobics for and that weight training? If you've got it, you've got to show it."

Donna could see that she wasn't making much impact on her friend. They belonged to two different traditions of black beauty. Carol belonged to the old school, but she was going to have to put on the new style if she was going to make any kind of impact on the dating scene.

"If you wanna look cool, you've got to wear something that's wild!"

Donna was too fast for the fashion industry, she didn't just wear the latest clothes but put them together in combinations that nobody had even thought about and before the designers picked up on it she had moved along to something else.

Carol knew that her flatmate believed in always being impeccably dressed and in shopping as hard for men as she did for her clothes. Donna was hung up on clothes and spent much of her time looking at and thinking about clothes and men, but Carol couldn't see how the men were treating her as anything but a sex object.

"Looking your best is important, you don't want to spend the rest of your life tied to a stove," Donna insisted. "When I was younger, I was the ugly duckling. I was the only black girl in an all white school outside Bristol. The other girls bullied me for no other reason than that I was bigger, blacker, taller, fatter and goofier than all the other girls. No boy would look at me, because I wore all the wrong clothes, so everybody laughed at me until I was 15, when things started to look up for me and boys suddenly started finding me attractive and suddenly I became really popular."

The two women had now been chatting and darting in and out of the tightly packed row of fashion shops on both sides of the road for nearly two hours. They must have been in and out of nearly every shop and though Donna was laden with a number of large shopping bags filled with the latest creations at knock down prices, Carol had still to make her choice. Finally, after a lot of deliberation, she chose a dress that made her look sensible but hardly sexy. Little did she know that Donna had slipped a really raunchy dress in Carol's size in amongst the others in Donna's shopping bags. One way or another, Donna had decided that she was going to make sure that her flat mate would have at least one dress in which men would find her irresistible!

Carol had been up all night working on a review of a new film for the local paper that she had clean forgotten that it was her birthday until she came down stairs in the morning and received the cards from Donna and Dee. It was a nice surprise, but being reminded of your birthday when you're 35, is hardly cause for celebration.

"Another year..." she said thoughtfully, "another reminder of how time is running by me."

"You're only thirty-five," Donna said. "That's no age at all. You're almost still a teenager."

"That's alright for you to say," Carol retorted. "You *are* almost a teenager. Wait until you hit thirty and you'll start to count the years left rather than how old you are."

Carol put a brave face on her new age. A birthday is easier to bear when you've got your best friends there to turn it into a celebration.

"So what do you want to do this evening?" Dee asked, "I'm coming home a bit earlier from work so that we could all maybe go out together."

Carol said that it would have been a good idea, the only thing was that she already had a date. Donna and

Dee were delighted for her. It was the first time Carol had been out in a long while.

"You go ahead and have that date," Dee urged, "don't worry about us, girl child. It's about time you went out meeting some men, show 'em what you got, honey."

"It's not exactly like that," Carol said, not to put too fine a point on it.

"Well, if you're not going to be here this evening, perhaps you better get your presents now."

Dee pulled out a little packet from her briefcase in the living room and presented it to Carol.

Inside a jewellry box, was an oversize necklace made out of beads and looking very African in effect.

"Oh I love this necklace," Carol said enthusiastically.

"It's not a necklace," Dee advised her, "it's a 'gri-gri' you wear that around your waist, next to your skin and you never take it off. It will protect you and keep you fertile and help you to realise your dreams. It's an old African thing..."

Carol lifted up her shirt and slipped the gri-gri around her waist.

"I can feel something happening already," she laughed.

"Don't mess with the spirits of our ancestors," Dee warned, "those things are for real."

Donna brought down a large package from her bedroom upstairs. As she unwrapped it, Carol's face broke into a smile as she recognised one of the most outrageous dresses that she and Donna had seen on Fonthill Road at the weekend. Donna had insisted that it would suit her perfectly, but Carol had declined, saying that she was too old for that type of thing and that in her day you would have been done for streaking in an outfit like it but it had been very sweet of her nevertheless to get it. Carol embraced Donna and kissed her on the cheek, but still insisted that she would never wear it outside the house. Dee urged her to put it on. Eventually Carol conceded. Both Donna and Dee thought she looked wicked with the gri-gri around her waist visible through the see-through top.

"All you need now is a brand new wide-brimmed hat and a pair of high heeled shoes and maybe some Ray Bans and you'll soon have those heads not only turning, but spinning around."

"I can't see any man resisting you looking like that," Dee agreed impressed, it really was the best she had seen her friend. Carol looked like a new woman a million miles from all her personal worries. Far from being a divorcee, she looked like a debutante coming out for the season.

Though the dress was nothing like she would have chosen herself, Carol couldn't help feeling that she looked fabulous wearing it.

It was Donna that came up with the idea.

"I know, let's have a party."

"Party for what?" Carol asked sceptically.

"Just a party, to celebrate.... let's have a house warming or whatever.... there doesn't have to be a reason does there? Let's just have a good, jamming party that people will be talking about for years to come. Let's invite all the decent men we know and all the single women we know, that's the recipe for success. Let's just have a party," Donna suggested.

Dee backed her up and said that she had not really been to a 'black man's' party in all the time she had been in London and it would be nice to compare how the British did things over here with the way they threw parties in the States. Carol was still sceptical, after all it was her house, she didn't know if it was a good idea having a lot of people she didn't even know traipsing around.

"Just give me some time to think about it," she said.

Dee snapped her briefcase shut and made her way out to work. Before departing, she turned around to Donna:

"Child, that wig looks damn foolish," she said frankly.

Donna shrugged her shoulders and flicked her long peroxide blonde wig.

"It ain't what you wear, it's how you wear it," she replied.

BLACK ENTERPRISE

The police finally found my Audi in Scotland after a week. Harvey had stolen the radio and all my new cassettes. At work, the general manager didn't seem too concerned about the loss of the car when I informed him. They were used to cars being stolen in England, especially in London, he explained.

"We've got the worst record in the world. Cars are stolen as often in this country as hamburgers are eaten in the States," he joked.

I thought it best not to mention the exact circumstances of the theft to anyone.

The new account I was working on promised to be the most interesting yet. Rex Publishing had moved over their advertising to Splash and made it clear that they had only done so because they had heard that Splash had a black woman account executive. I remembered that Andre had mentioned that they were his publishers and the first thing I said when I met the two young black men who owned the company was that I knew one of their authors.

"Oh Andre?" said Devon, the taller, darker partner, "yeah, wicked author. He's going places. Give him some time and he'll end up being one of the most successful authors in America. Wait and see."

It was mostly with the more laid back other partner, Simon that I dealt with on the account. He was the business half of the partnership and seemed to know a lot about advertising and what he wanted the agency to do

131

for Rex Publishing.

"We're 'the publisher with attitude'," he explained, so we've got to have memorable adverts even if it upsets some people."

I had a great two weeks, reading through the range of Rex Publishing books — I had finished Andre's in a week — which Simon had sent to me so I could come up with some ideas. I hadn't read black fiction like this before, not even in the States. It was snappy, exciting, entertaining and a great read. I couldn't wait to get started properly on the project, this was going to be fun.

Once I had read the books I called Simon on the mobile number he had given me.

"Which book did you like best?" he asked when I told him how much I had enjoyed reading them.

"It's got to be *Pickney*," I replied. "I really liked the Vincent Kelly gangster books, but I'm not so familiar with the type of life he writes about. But *Pickney* was a really universal topic."

"But you got an idea about the type of books we publish," he continued. "What we want you to do on this advertising campaign is to continually assure our readers that when they see our logo they are buying the genuine article and not a fake by one of our competitors. The important thing is to develop brand loyalty amongst our readers."

I had thought about the campaign and suggested that they should continue to advertise their product exclusively in the black media — cable television, pirate radio stations and the one or two black legal stations, and print media as well as their street posters.

"But maybe the design on the adverts could be improved."

Simon agreed and said that he had designed their

advertising himself though he wasn't really a designer.

"I'll tell you what, Dee, I'll leave everything in your hands. Give me a call when you're ready to show me something on paper and I'll take you out to lunch to discuss things. How does that sound?"

I said it sounded fine.

I had already insisted on the art director taking a holiday, he was serving no purpose staring dreamily into thin air at work every day anyway. The Rex Publishing account gave me an opportunity to test out a young black designer who had brought his portfolio in for me to see the previous week. He was only too keen to come in and work on the project on a freelance basis and he had already read all Rex Publishing's books which made things easier. Marc was only 21, heavy set with a goatee and dressed like a cross between an art student and a be-bop jazz musician. But given the opportunity, he proved to be a really talented designer with great ideas and so conversant with the Apple Macintosh computer's QuarkXPress design programme that he worked fast, too fast sometimes and didn't understand that he couldn't spend the rest of the time chatting to his girlfriend on the telephone, even though the agency was paying him an hourly rate.

I returned home late from work one Tuesday evening to find Carol's copy of The Voice sprawled out across the coffee table in the living room. As per usual she had left some of her home made low-fat oatmeal raisin cookies on a plate for me. She wasn't around and neither was Donna. I was tired but didn't feel like going up to bed. there was nothing interesting on the television either, so I settled down to reading the week's news in 'Britain's Best Black Newspaper'. I flicked through the pages — the letters page, the Tony Sewell column, Sister Marcia's gospel page and through the entertainment section and the women's page. I finally came to the 'Heart To Heart' dating page and scanned through the ads, there were always some cheeky ones:

SEE ME YAH 6' 1", handsome male, athletic, witty, passionate, 26, G.S.O.H., seeks romantic, affectionate, humourous female to become one in mind, body and soul.

FULL-FIGURED, plump, black woman, size 18 or over, needed by attractive, professional, mixed race male, 45, for fun-loving, long-term relationship. London area.

WANT KIDS SOON? Crazy, tall black male seeks adventurous, young girlfriend. Laughter and cuddles essential. All nationalities welcome. Pregnant girl considered. London-ish. Write before it's too late.

EVER DREAMED of a caring, professional, witty, mouth-watering, black British male, 32, who'd appreciate your every embodiment of femininity? Why dream? Harmony awaits you. A.L.A.W.P.

SEXY RAGGA man, 25, with own flat and lonely seeks 'fit' ragga lady. Must be over 25, 5' 9". Call me, let's flex! Jamaican/English only.

ATTRACTIVE, black hunk, 30, lonely but not desperate, seeks confident, level-headed, employed, childless, caring black woman to share life's ups and downs.

SPORTY black male, 50+, seeks lively ethnic or mixed race companion for two weeks jaunt to Spain in Oct/Nov. Interested?

CAN you make up for lost years? Single Nigerian male, 26, enslaved for years by loneliness and inactivity seeks liberation. N/S female, 20-30.

I'M A PLAYFUL, slim, 28, coppertop, widower and don't like being on my own. I gotta lot to give to the right woman.

AGROPHOBIC black male, 30, seeks female company, any nationality, for intimate dates in tiny bedroom. All replies answered.

IRRESISTIBLE large, damned fine black man, 29, looking for love, affection and a good woman who enjoys life. Midlands/London.

PROFESSIONAL white male, 32, 5' 11", fit, seeking sexy, feminine, dark Jamaican lady, with weave-on, painted nails, batty riders and tall boots, who wants lasting love.

EARTHBOUND astronaut, own rocket, young crew, heading to stars and galaxies beyond, awaiting space-woman, 25-35, 5' 7"+, for long-term cosmic travel. Countdown commencing.

GOOD LOOKING, professional, black male,28, tired of giving, willing to share, seeks employed, conscious, classy, intelligent, cultured, black beauty. Christian values.

STILL, looking? Educated, employed, 'street-wise', well-endowed, 5' 7"+, 25+, childless, African/mixed race beauty? Enjoy mental, physical, aesthetic escapades? music? 'Black issues'? Black engineer, 5' 8", 30+ needs you.

TALL black man, 35, seeks slim, attractive woman to share time and space, confidence and positive attitude more important than age.

SITTING on the dock of the bay watching the tide... Black male, 43. Want to waste time with me? You: gorgeous, sexy black woman. Birmingham area.

ALL this love going to waste, it's a crime. Someone should arrest this pale prince, 31, bring him to justice. Reward includes diverse qualities.

BLACK male, 25, 'uncut diamond', seeks black female 20-25, to help him polish off his rough edges. Ladies are you up to the challenge?

It wasn't easy regaining an interest in dating again after my experience with Harvey. But reading other people's dating messages was one more reminder that I was 30-years-old, had everything going for me and in a foreign country, yet single. However much I enjoyed being in London, I knew deep down that I wouldn't be happy unless that emptiness in my romantic life was filled with someone permanent. One of the adverts caught my eye and ready to try anything once, a thought crossed my mind:

MALE, black, professional, slim, tall, 29, handsome and a

gentleman, seeks 'likewise' female. Strong, gentle, solvent, quietly confident, for friendship and going out on social occasions.

Without thinking about it too much, I dialled the toll number underneath, more out of curiosity than anything else but also because I thought it would be good to have one black male friend who didn't want anything from me, but whose company I enjoyed on a platonic basis. I listened to the man's polished English accent on the tape-recorded message interestedly.

"Hi, my name is Trevor. Thank you for responding to my advert. I shall be brief, because my advert says it all. If you're an open-minded and adventurous black woman with a career who enjoys the high life but are tired of going to concerts, the movies or the theatre by yourself, then leave your number and I'll get back to you. If you're the right woman, we'll soon be enjoying a pleasant 'no strings attached' date in town. You'll find me interesting, widely-read, intelligent, good company and thoroughly professional. So don't waste time, leave your number."

Without thinking about it, I left my number, then regretted it almost immediately, but it was too late.

Trevor called about an hour later. I was surprised but interested. He seemed eager to meet up. He said that there was a new Wesley Snipes film showing at the Electric Cinema in West London. I agreed that it sounded like a good idea and we decided to meet outside on Portobello Road. I would be carrying a copy of Newsweek magazine and he said he would be carrying a copy of The Journal.

The next evening, I hurried to West London by tube. I got to the cinema on time and had only stood outside for a moment when a short Spike Lee — lookalike with thick-rimmed glasses and wearing a New York Knicks baseball cap, stuck his head out of a beaten up old Japanese car parked by the sidewalk, waving a copy of The Voice and The Journal.

"You must be Dee," he said with a broad grin, pointing to my copy of Newsweek. "Hi, I'm Trevor," he said, climbing out of the car and stretching out his hand to greet me.

I looked him up and down, unable to believe that he was the same guy who had described himself so appealingly in the advert. Trevor saw the expression of puzzlement on my face and explained:

"Yeah, I know," he began, "the paper made a mistake and mixed my description up with somebody else's. There was nothing I could do about it. I wondered why he hadn't corrected the mistake on the answering machine or told me on the telephone that he didn't match the description of himself as advertised and he assured me that he had only just seen the mistake on his way to meet me when he picked up a copy of The Voice at the newsagent.

I wasn't totally convinced, though he seemed earnest. I had the option of turning around and going home, but didn't want to diss him if he was telling the truth. Besides, I had psyched myself up to fantasise with Wesley on the big screen in front of me for ninety minutes and what harm could it do to just have a social date with a man I didn't feel the least bit attracted to?

I made a point of going Dutch with him. The last thing I wanted was for Trevor to feel in any way that he had 'invested' anything in me by paying for the tickets. As we sat through the commercials waiting for the feature to begin, he explained that he was an engineer for British

Telecom, but he had only recently been relocated to London from a small town on the south coast.

"Coming to London to work is like a big adventure," he enthused, "but I haven't found many people who I really want to go out and have a good time with, you know what I mean?"

I said I did. I was in the same situation after all. The one thing I didn't say was that I *still* hadn't found anybody who I really wanted to go out and have a good time with in London.

Trevor did most of the talking. He had an irritating habit of reading my lips when I spoke, following my words and finishing off my sentences at the same time as I did. But I didn't mention it.

"I love films," he said, "I've seen thousands of them, but I don't like watching them on video, you know what I mean? It's not the same thing. So what's your favourite film? Mine is Casablanca with Humphrey Bogart. I mean it's got everything, hasn't it? It's got the thriller and romance elements — and you're not going to see a much more thrilling or romantic film — and of course it's got the music with old 'play it again Sam' — the token black man — playing it again, every now and then... and then Bogart and Bacall, what a team, eh?"

As much as I wanted to take Trevor seriously, I was past being excited about meeting up with him and couldn't help feeling more than a tinge of disappointment that he was nothing like I had expected. Worse still, when a couple of cinemagoers brushed passed us to get to their seats beyond where we were sitting in the aisle, they knocked Trevor's baseball cap off accidently, revealing a shiny, bald head with hair only on the sides and back! I tried to concentrate on the movie and Wesley up there on the screen for the rest of the time.

I already knew when I said my goodbyes that evening that I wouldn't be seeing Trevor again. I had run my minimum requirements through my mind so many times that I knew exactly the type of man I wanted to socialise with, and Trevor wasn't he. He had to be cute, ambitious and charismatic and he had to be sincere. I was looking for a real professional, even just to socialise with, someone on my level, not a telephone engineer.

Trevor had my home number however, and for the next two weeks lay siege on our telephone, leaving messages on the machine and with Donna and Carol for me. I never returned his calls and he eventually stopped ringing.

The day finally came when I had to make my presentation to Rex Publishing. Simon sent his chauffeur down to pick me up and I was driven in the silver Mercedes to a nice Caribbean restaurant in Chalk Farm where Simon was already waiting to have lunch. I hadn't been to Cottons before and was thrilled and delighted as I looked about me that the other diners were almost exclusively black professionals. We shared a 'Belly Nah Bawl' meal for two after which I showed him the portfolio. He went against every one of the suggestions. He wanted the company logo written larger and he wanted a different colour scheme. He didn't see things the way I did at all and felt the series of photos of black celebrities with their favourite Rex novel captioned underneath, was the wrong approach.

"Just because Jane Public has bought a product in a certain way in the past doesn't mean she's going to continue doing it that way, does it?" he said. "Our readers trust our product because they know we publish entertaining contemporary black fiction, so we should have photos of those readers, the ordinary people, with their favourite books."

I fought for my ideas as hard as I could and protested that celebrities were the best way to sell a product that I really knew what I was doing and that they had to look at the whole thing on a long term basis, but he wasn't convinced. In the end I conceded that he was right.

"To be honest, I have a deep disrespect for advertising agencies," he said. "I sometimes wonder if I couldn't do the whole thing myself, it's just the time factor that stops me. But I suppose you hear that from all your clients?"

I nodded.

"Especially when we present them with the bill."

Simon smiled.

"Dee, I hope you're not one of those typical ad people, who lives, eats and breathes advertising. I hope you're able to go out and enjoy yourself as well."

"Sure," I said, "all the time."

It wasn't the truth but in advertising you learn to say the things the client wants to hear. I continued using my fork to pick at the curried vegetables and rice on the combination platter.

"So which kind of clubs have you been to since you've been in London? Have you been to Moonlighting? The Roof Garden? Gantons?"

I admitted that I hadn't yet been out to let my hair down properly, but had mostly been to the movies or to the theatre when I had time.

"But that's because I haven't really discovered where black professionals hang out."

"Well, you must come along to this little party one of our authors is having at his place on Saturday. I think you'll like it if you're interested in meeting black professionals. I'll tell you what, why don't I come by to pick you up about seven on Saturday evening?"

Simon didn't have to ask me twice, because as much as I wanted to meet a crowd of 'my kinda people', I was also daydreaming of getting to know Simon 'off-duty'.

MOUTH TO MOUTH

Janice and Ollie finally arrived to collect the kids. Martin and Shannon knew that they could get away with anything when they were at their aunt's house and that she always spoiled them. Despite the fact that their mother had expressly told them and her sister that they weren't to have any sweets, they were able to sulk enough until Carol conceded that one ice cream wouldn't do any harm and they had taken a walk down to the local newsagent where Martin was quick to choose the largest and most expensive ice cream in the freezer, while his sister selected her favourite, which was somewhat cheaper. If Carol thought however, that she was going to get peace and quiet after the bribe, she was mistaken. That was just the beginning. Once they knew they could get away with almost anything with their aunt, they set about turning the house upside down, fighting with each other and playing their aunt off with one another. Six-year-old Martin was clever far beyond his years. He didn't understand fully what it meant that his cousin Junior had died the previous year, he was too young, but it hadn't escaped his attention that his aunt now doted on him as if he was her own son. He looked forward to going around to Auntie Carol's, it was like Christmas every time. Ten-year-old Shannon understood. She missed Junior also and tried her best to be a good girl whenever her aunt babysat. But she was a tomboy and couldn't resist joining in with her brother if he chose to kick his football around in the conservatory. What she found most enjoyable was teasing her younger brother by flexing her greater strength until he started a fight which she would always win. It wasn't that she enjoyed seeing him cry and bawl out for his Auntie, because she truly loved him. It was just that she wanted to show him who was boss.

"Unnnnnnnnnghhh!" Martin wailed, tears streaming down his face.

Carol looked up and shook her head.

"What is it this time?" she asked impatiently.

"Auntie Carol..." Martin began slowly and purposefully, stressing every syllable and gasping for air in between, "Sha...nnon took...ungggghhh...my foot...unnnngggghhh...ball from me..unnnggghhh... an' she says she won't give...unnnggghhh...it back to me unt...il I'm big e...unnnnggghhhh...nuff to take it... Unnnnnnnnggggggggghhh!"

"Shannon!" Carol called out, "give Martin back his ball and give it back to him now."

"What!!!" Shannon cried out from the top of the stairs, pretending that she couldn't hear a word.

"I said give him back his ball... Do you hear me?!"

"Sorry Auntie," Shannon called back, "I think I've gone deaf... I can't hear anything you're saying."

"Shannon!!!" This time there was threat in her Aunt's voice and the little child threw her brother's ball back to him."

"He's such a baby!" the young girl called out.

Carol lay her head back on the sofa. She was tired. She thought about Junior and wished he was here to play with his cousins. Having Shannon and Martin around for the evening had made her yearn for her own child. Well, Junior was with God now, there was nothing she could do about that, but would she ever get the chance to mother another child?

At that moment the doorbell rang and Martin rushed to the door to open up for his mother and father.

"Daddy, daddy! Look what Auntie Carol gave me," Martin cried out as his parents stepped in, proudly displaying the watch that his aunt had bought him.

"Oh Carol... you're going to end up spoiling that child you know," Ollie said.

He was a tall and powerfully built British-born Grenadian of 29 years who lived for his wife and family first and foremost.

"I have told her that," Janice quipped. "You better take care of that watch, Martin," she turned to her son, "because you're not going to get another one."

"And you better learn the time quick," Martin's father added, "because from now on, I'm not going to use my watch again, I'm just going to be asking you the time."

"I know how to tell the time," Martin said with a cheeky smile.

"No he doesn't," Shannon teased, "silly boy doesn't even know his times table...hahaha!"

Martin turned to his sister and without hesitation, kicked her squarely on the shin. "Yes I do!" he insisted.

Shannon screamed as loudly as she could.

"What did you just do?" Ollie asked his son incredulously. Martin simply rested his hands on his hips and stood his ground defiantly.

"You are not looking at me like that, are you?" his father asked.

Martin knew who he shouldn't mess with. He dropped his hands by his side. Shannon continued screaming as if she were about to die.

"Alright, alright!" Janice comforted her, "don't overdo it Shannon, or we'll have to take you to the hospital..."

"I want to go to the hospital," Shannon cried through her wailing.

"Well you're not going," her mother countered, "so you better get well quickly. We've got to go home..."

She took her daughter by the hand and Shannon quietened her down.

Ollie was still dealing with Martin.

"We've been standing here for two minutes and you still haven't apologised to your sister."

"But she started it," Martin appealed.

"I don't care who started what," Ollie said, "where do you get off kicking your sister? Who taught you that? You've got five seconds to apologise to her and I'm talking a real apology, because you've just done something to your sister which you should be ashamed of."

Martin took his full five seconds, but when he apologised, he went over to his sister and kissed her on the cheek.

"I'm sorry Shannon."

He thought about it for another second, then he hugged his sister. "I love you."

Shannon hugged her brother back.

"And I'm sorry also, Martin."

"I'm sorry about all this, Carol," Janice said. "Have they been troublesome?"

"They've been alright. I wish I had your problems."

"Not with these two you don't," Janice assured. "You don't know the half of it. You don't have to live with them full-time."

"So how was the show?" Carol asked.

"It was really good," Ollie said, nodding. "You should go and see it."

Janice and Ollie had been out to see a production of

Carmen Jones at a theatre in East London. The production starred a UK-based soap opera star, who had had rave reviews for her interpretation of the classic musical. Carol took down the details of the theatre and said she would consider going to see it.

"But you're going to have to go on your own," her sister said, "because you done scared away every eligible man this side of London."

"Not every man..." Carol protested.

"Oh so, don't tell me that things have turned out sweet between you and Dalton? I don't believe it."

"Nothing like that," Carol smiled.

"No, I can tell it from your eyes," Janice countered."You do like him, don't you? You actually like him." She laughed. "Well good for you."

Ollie coughed. The kids were getting fidgety again anyway and they had their beds to go home to.

"I'll call you tomorrow," Janice insisted. "I want to know all the juicy bits."

From the doorstep Carol waved goodbye to her sister and family as they roared off in their Volvo estate.

Everything seemed quiet in the house once the children had gone. Suddenly, Carol was full of energy again and she decided to make the phone call she had been considering making all day.

"Hi Dalton, it's me," she said.

"Hi. What are you doing?" came the jovial reply down the phone.

"Nothing, I just thought I'd call to see how you were."

"You can call me any time," Dalton said.

If he had thought he was about to get off with his date when she suddenly turned around and started kissing him in the taxi cab on their first meeting, Dalton had another thing coming. Once the cab pulled off from the lights, Carol completely withdrew her advances. When he pressed her, she couldn't deny that she had enjoyed the embrace. Neither did she deny that she wanted to do it again, but when he made an attempt to resume, she stopped him and said she just wanted friendship and that he was pushing their intimacy too fast. He asked her whether it was because she found him unattractive. She said "no". "Average then?"

"No, I think you're very attractive."

It had been so long since she had been so intimate with anyone, that feeling Dalton's warm breath in her mouth as his tongue toyed sensitively with hers had reminded her of how much she had missed having someone who could make her feel secure, but also excite her at the same time. Like any other woman she needed a big hug every now and then to make her feel she was the most important person in the world. And being in a position where she was meeting available young black men was preferable to staying at home moping. She was pleased that he took an interest in her, but Carol just couldn't bring herself to trust a man a hundred percent again after Neville. Anyway, it was never too late to get 'dirty' with Dalton, men never 'just say no' and if a woman offers sex, even despite the fact that they may want to wait, they always say yes.

"I've got a few questions to ask you," Carol continued down the phone line.

"Sounds intriguing," Dalton replied. "Don't you trust me yet?"

He was getting used to it. He had now dated Carol twice and both times he had felt like he was under interrogation. As well as that, they were always spending time discussing things over the phone, but they never ended up doing anything.

Carol responded that she was entitled to question him. She had already made her mistakes in life and couldn't afford to befriend a man she didn't know.

"Fire away!" Dalton said confidently.

"Who did you make love to last night, a girlfriend or a casual acquaintance?"

The line went silent for a moment, before Dalton let out a loud laugh.

"How can you ask me that? What do you expect me to say?"

"The truth," Carol said unamused. "You've got nothing to hide from me, it's not like we're having an affair. Or can't you even be honest with your friends?"

"I slept in my bed alone last night," Dalton answered with a sigh.

"And the night before?"

"Same thing."

"When was the last time you made love?"

Dalton dodged the question as much as he could, said that Carol was going too far, and anyway it had been such a long time ago, he couldn't remember."

"Try," Carol insisted.

"Well... I suppose after my wife left me, I went a bit crazy... spite sex, you understand... I don't know, maybe six months ago."

"So what have you been doing since then?"

"What???!"

"You know, you're a man... How have you been satisfying yourself since then? Do you masturbate?"

Dalton laughed a laugh of embarrassment.

"I can't believe this, I'm 38 years old, I'm an accountant. You think I've got time to spend pulling at my plunger every night?"

"There's nothing wrong with it. Everyone knows that

everyone does..."

"Well, let me ask you a question, do you masturbate?"

"When I have to."

The line went silent again.

"Why don't we just get it on?" Dalton asked finally. "You don't need to do those things, Carol. Why don't you just pick up the phone when you're feeling lonely, and call me?"

Carol had wondered the same thing herself. It seemed so easy and yet out of the question. She was waiting until the right time for sex in their relationship. She was more likely to have sex with a partner she loved and she just didn't know about Dalton.

He seemed nice enough, the type of man who would pull out her chair for her and hold the car door for her - always. He was a professional and had both education and social status. But did she like him enough to make love to him? Or did she just want friendship? She would have to postpone sex with Dalton until she was sure. Her husband's behaviour had seen to that.

Neville had made her less interested in sex. When he first started becoming distant after Junior's birth, she attempted to be better at sex, because she had read in a woman's magazine that having a good sexual relationship was the best defence against your partner playing away from home. When they made love, she made sure she always asked him what he enjoyed and ways in which she could make the sex for him even better. But sex was a poor consolation for her real needs which was a desire for intimacy. Neville however had enjoyed the opportunity to try out new and varied sexual experiences with his wife.

Back on the phone, Dalton said that postponing sex

didn't decrease the extent of the feelings he had for her. Anyway, why didn't she come around to his place for dinner at the weekend? She accepted as long as sex was not on the menu. He said that it was a good job he was old enough to remember her old fashioned attitude but that the "make them wait" approach would not go down too well with a lot of other men. She said goodbye, but before replacing the receiver, added that if he couldn't just be friends he was obviously not the type of man she needed.

Two days later, Carol received a formal invitation to dinner from Dalton. He had taken a leaf out of Janice's book:

You are invited to my house for a night of romance. The evening will begin with dinner and drinks and conclude with a classic romantic movie... There will be absolutely no sex on the menu. No cancellations allowed. Dress formally.

Dalton lived in a beautiful three bedroomed maisonette above a bank on Camden High Street. The apartment was huge, particularly the attic living room which opened out to a beautiful roof top patio filled with tall plants in huge pots. Carol was suitably impressed.

"I got it really cheap a few years ago when the prices were low," he explained, ready with a glass of champagne for Carol after taking her raincoat.

They sat to a pleasant candle-lit meal of fresh pasta and spinach with caviar, courtesy of the local Sainsbury's, Dalton admitted.

"I know what you're feeling," Dalton said suddenly as they ate. "Remember, my partner left me also. And when you were together with someone as long as we were, you never really forget them. One thing I've learned is that you can't keep torturing yourself. You've got to start a new life. If you find someone special, take my advice and hold him tight. Don't be stingy with your affections."

He paused briefly, studying Carol for her reaction and then he told his story:

"I used to come home from work, give my wife a brief kiss and sit down to dinner without realising that she was in a bad mood. I just assumed that because we were together and she wasn't nagging, everything was alright. I thought that the more I could afford to buy her, the more she would love me. Boy was I wrong."

"It's a fabulous place," Carol said again as she helped him to clear the table after dinner. Dalton admitted that it felt huge since his wife had walked out. He was always trying to find uses for the two extra bedrooms now that he wasn't going to have kids in the forseeable future.

Before setting up the video, he cooked some popcorn in a pan. Carol rummaged through his larder busily, looking for ingredients. She said that she could knock something up quickly which would go well with popcorn. Dalton looked on in awe as she prepared her famous caramel topping.

"Absolutely delicious," Dalton said, having dipped his finger in the sauce for a taste, then he hit the lights and they snuggled up cozily in front of the fireplace to watch an old Sidney Poitier film.

It was the most romantic evening Carol had experienced for years. She didn't need a man with diamonds and rings of 18 carat gold, because that would never last; what she needed was a big, strong hand to lift her to a higher level and make her feel like a queen. A romantic evening like this brings you close to another, whether you wanted it or not. If she and Neville had had evenings like this they would have been able to sit down and work out any other problems in their lives.

"Just answer me one thing," Dalton began after the movie, "do you consider me as just a friend or am I a bit more than that?"

Carol looked at him long and hard, her resistance was almost broken.

"Just a bit more than that."

"I hope so, because I'm fed up with talking to my cat all the time."

Dalton had rolled out the spare futon and spread a blanket on top for them to lie on. Carol looked at her watch and said she had better be going, but it was only a half-hearted suggestion. Instead, she agreed to Dalton filling up her champagne glass once more. For the next hour, the two lay on the futon, having intimate discussions, but nothing more, with Joyce Sims singing *Come Into My Life* softly in the background. Slowly, they began touching each other and then caressing and gently petting, but mostly they talked. They gave themselves enough time to lounge and laugh and in a way, learn to love in bed.

He said that he had strong feelings for her and that he was going to do everything in his power to make their time together the most beautiful, the most warm and the most intimate of any relationship and that they should not try to manipulate or control each other

"I vow to support and nurture this relationship through its growth and changes. I promise to be there for you always."

"As far as I am concerned you can never say 'I love you' too often," she said, finally allowing him to come into her life. She had *so* much love to show him. She wanted to inspire him with her love. She wanted love to create an 'us' and not to destroy the 'me' that was there.

Before they went any further, Dalton hit the tape button and out through the speakers, the sound of Mozart filled the room.

"This stuff is great for making love to," he said, joining her again on the futon.

"Did you see that TV documentary on AIDS? That stuff is dread."

The question stopped Dalton in his tracks, coming as it did out of the blue.

"How has the fear of AIDS changed your sexual behaviour? What are you doing to protect yourself from catching AIDS?" she asked.

She had been meaning to bring up the topic earlier, without making him feel a way to find out if he was in a high risk category. But before she was able to raise the topic, she had found herself in this compromising position where he was hard to resist.

He reasserted that he had been as good as celibate in the last six months and that she had nothing to worry about.

Nevertheless, she insisted, "no glove, no love." Besides she had sickle cell trait, her son had died of sickle cell anaemia and to make a mistake with Dalton without a blood check would be criminal.

It didn't take long for Dalton to 'conjure' some up from the bathroom downstairs.

When they made love he handled her body like a valuable musical instrument, following the classical music's highs and lows. He started off fast and passionately and wound-down to a conclusion, soft and gentle, breathless and light. The Jupiter Symphony No 41 had four movements. The first was strong, passionate and energetic and it soon got them going. They slowed the pace right down as the second movement came up... By the end of the third movement, they were both moaning ecstatically as the symphony came to a resounding close. Exhausted, they lay still, side by side, both staring up at the ceiling. Neither had anything more to add.

DICKIE INSPECTION

With each new partner the possibility that this could be Mr Right is always at the back of your mind, especially if he's a good lover, good looking, good natured and good value. That's why a lot of single black women like me keep shopping around and wondering, should I get involved, can I trust him, is he worth it? Alex puts it down to 'cock fixation', that I can't get enough. But then a man would say that wouldn't he, rather than accept that he ain't adequate.

Reggie over-rated his penis. Making sure I had several orgasms every time became too important and he was always trying out new positions such as the 'roast duck' and 'the stag' to make sure that I got a satisfyingly good bed-work. If I wasn't ecstatic he behaved as if his penis had let him down and like he was only half the man he was.

You could loosely describe me as his 'woman' as I had dated him a few times now. But he kept stressing that he was too much of a sex symbol for his female fans to find out that he was with one particular woman, so our relationship was never 'official'. I became an 'accessory' to him whenever he needed to appear at an event. If you want to be noticed, you get yourself a stunning date as well as a flash car and clothes. Reggie could afford to have a stunning girl as just another asset or status symbol.

I was accompanying him to an 'exclusive' party later that evening, so in my bedroom beforehand it was a case of 'wham, bam , thank you ma'am' but that was just not good enough for me. If a man couldn't turn me on, I wasn't interested.

When we made love he moved so fast that I didn't have a chance to come, but I didn't want to say so for fear of bruising his ego. As soon as he entered me he transformed into a Grand National jockey — with his sights fixed on crossing that finish line before anybody else. Then he rolled over on his side, sweating, exhausted. After a while he opened his watery eyes slowly and panted:

"How was it for you?"

I simply smiled, looking into his eyes deeply.

"You came didn't you?"he asked.

I had to stifle a laugh. Sure, I came I nodded ironically, sure I came.

"I knew it, I could feel it... it was great."

Like most men my age, 24, he thought that being good in bed was the most important requirement of a relationship. Reggie took his cock far too seriously. He always had to convince himself that he was a real stud, (drinking more than anybody else, smoking the most ganja too). And when he's in that mood I can't really get close to him because he's too busy thinking about his dick all the time. It was as if he lived to perpetuate the image of the Jamaican man as ever-hard and ever-ready, even though he was 'Mr Once All Night'.

I would have to put him right, teach him a thing or two about tenderness, warmth, emotion and closeness. Quite simply I had to teach him about love, a foreign concept to Reggie.

I rarely volunteered to have oral sex with any man, but Reggie had asked so many times and I felt it might arouse his interest. So I decided to allow him this one moment of pleasure. He lay his muscled body back on the bed, our eyes locked momentarily. Very slowly I began licking his penis. The warmth of my mouth stimulated him immediately and his manhood stood erect. I slipped the penis head into my mouth gently and teased with the tip of my tongue darting around under the edge of the rim. Eventually I took the whole penis into my mouth carefully, sucking it and moving my lips up and down the sturdy shaft as Reggie sighed repeatedly with pleasure, murmuring, "Yes, oh yes... oh yes, oh yes, oh yes..." I couldn't have got the whole penis into my mouth without gagging, so I held the base of it with a hand, stroking it rapidly up and down and with my other hand fondled his balls lightly. Reggie began to breathe heavily, his pelvis jerking to a rhythm of its own and his balls dancing around uncontrollably. I knew that I had only thirty seconds, maybe a minute. I moved my mouth rapidly up and down and then quickly pulled out just before a spray of semen and a long, mournful sigh attested to the pleasure Reggie had enjoyed.

Whatever he said otherwise, I knew he didn't love me, he was just enjoying the thrill of being a hot pop star with women falling over him all over the place. But I was getting what I needed out of the relationship. Through dating Reggie, I was meeting all sorts of people who could be useful in my career. I figured I could handle being his status symbol, and if I couldn't I'd get out quickly.

Sleeping with Alex was preferable, though he was less experienced. Yes, I was still sleeping with Alex the way you do with a good friend who you know isn't the right man for you, but you're so intimate with anyway that sex doesn't feel bad. I wouldn't even know if he was sexually aroused when I dropped by his tiny apartment, until I noticed his penis getting hard as we sat down to drink coffee. He wouldn't know it either from the look on his face, until he felt his jeans becoming tight. He didn't want to admit that I was able to control him with sex, but it was true. I had the power in the relationship and was able to bend him over backwards for me. Though Reggie didn't know I was sleeping with Alex, Alex knew about Reggie and though he wasn't overjoyed, he accepted that he was my 'bit on the side' and that I would date other people, as long as I never stopped coming around to see him.

I felt bad about the situation but I was only getting half of what I needed from each of them and I didn't want to dump either.

I always felt close to Alex, he was the sweetest man I had known. I was relaxed and myself with him and I enjoyed talking to him for hours before and after sex.

"What do you enjoy most about kissing my body?" I asked him as we both lay naked on his mattress.

He paused for a moment just as he was applying his lips gently to the base of my spine.

He replied that my body was like a cure for his love sickness.

Reggie had promised that he would have me on his next video and I had been eager for him to get back from tour, so shooting could start.

He came around to our house as soon as he got back from tour. He said he knew where his duty lay and was ready to give his woman the "good bed-work," so we got straight to it. I tended to his penis by mounting him, facing his feet as we rocked the bed during intercourse, massaging his inner thigh and tickling his balls while his cock was safe and warm inside of me. Though Reggie was stiff and hard to start off with, he quickly went soft —

to his embarrassment.

"Just because I don't have a hard on doesn't mean that I'm not horny," he said dismissively, when I wondered why he wasn't interested. "That's the problem with women, they think if a man hasn't got a hard on, there's something wrong! If a limp dick is the worst thing in your relationship, you're livin' large. Cho! It's not easy having a cock that's out of control, y'know. I don't know what's wrong, it gets hard when I'm on stage or driving in my jeep... but you're not around then and by the time I get round here, it's gone."

I was thinking, "This man doesn't find me attractive anymore — that's why he's got a limp dick. Okay, his dick wasn't working but there were lots of other ways he could interest me sexually. Why couldn't he give me a back rub? Why couldn't he go downtown on me?

It was the same thing the next two times we met up. After that second time, Reggie broke down crying and told me how he wished women would stop wanting him just for sex. The 'G-Spot' gimmick had been taken too literally because now women were only interested in the novelty of sleeping with him. He almost felt he had to get married just to get away from his image.

From that evening on, my whirlwind romance with Reggie began to fade.

I always ended up choosing the same type of men over and over, some of whom did and some of whom didn't satisfy my needs. When Reggie found out that he wasn't able to get his dick up he was so embarrassed he just disappeared. He also changed his mobile number, so I couldn't get hold of him for weeks. When I finally did, he just said, "Look, I'm busy." I figured that I had been dropped. When I asked him if all this was because he couldn't get it up, he got very angry and shouted down the line that it was because he couldn't date a woman who was a sell out to her race and thought she was white and walked around with a blonde wig.

"You're beautiful baby, just beautiful!" Colin coaxed as he peered down the lens of his camera at me. I was dressed in a Calvin Klein see-through slip dress that was falling off one shoulder and a white micro-bikini underneath, barely able to contain my figure and my hair was pulled back.

I had decided to concentrate on modelling. There was no point in waiting to get more work on Reggie's videos, so I turned to Colin who didn't seem to mind that I was no longer Reggie's woman. He was still prepared to help me and thought I had a good chance of making it as a model. He said he enjoyed working with me because I had a beauty and shape which was unique and because unlike other models I always knew which make up to use for which occasion and which dresses to wear.

"I'm going to take these photos to a friend of mine," Colin said. "His agency are looking for some sexy black women for a catalogue. I'm sure they'll love these shots."

Long gone were the days when using a black face on a product in Britain was unthinkable. On the contrary, agencies were now actively looking for black models. Because now it was acknowledged that black kids, black women and black men set the trends which everybody else follows. Multi-national clothes companies were now actively seeking the seal of approval for their products from the black community. Car companies wanted a sexy black woman to sell their cars and phone companies were using upwardly mobile black females to sell their services. They had finally discovered that they weren't going to make any money without the respect of the black community.

"Just do what you think is best!" I told Colin. I trusted him and had regarded him as a photographing friend who I could talk to, since we met that first night in the night club.

He continued clicking away as fast as he could. My every twitch was captured for posterity with the help of a motor at the bottom of his camera, which increased the shutter speed to the rapid fire of an automatic pistol. Several rolls of film later he was still not finished.

"Okay, keep that smile...." he said, "that's brilliant... really brilliant.... yeah hold it for a couple more.... that's incredible."

At the end of the session, Colin promised to get together a contact sheet of the best shots and allow me to choose from them any prints I wanted personally.

"Just one thing," he said, grabbing my wrist just as I was about to disappear behind the screen in the studio to get changed, "Reggie said that you give really good head and he doesn't mind if you give me the same, 'on the house'."

JUST WANNA HAVE FUN

The idea for the party came from Donna's favourite rap video in which everyone dressed up as characters from seventies blaxploitation films. She suggested that the housemates went out and bought a huge Afro wig each and that their guests should do the same. Dee was up for it and added that they ought to go the whole way by shopping for some fluorescent mini skirts, satin hot pants and thigh-high go-go boots. It would be a costume party where everybody had to dress seventies style! The men in flared trousers and the women in hot pants or minis.

Carol frowned and said that she was just old enough to have dated guys in bell bottoms and huge Afros. She didn't think she could take the whole thing seriously, but she would go along with it. It was settled then. They would throw an unforgettable party. Dee got to work designing and getting some invites printed up. Donna did her bit by sorting out the music. She had enough contacts in the business to sort out a free sound for the night. Carol also contributed by calling up all her girlfriends, some of whom she hadn't seen for years. Many of them were attached, but agreed to come as 'single'. It was difficult choosing which men to invite. They told all their girlfriends to invite men who they themselves weren't interested in to meet other women. The requirement was that they would invite men who to their knowledge had never dissed a woman, but they as hostesses wouldn't invite any of the men they were dating either. There was no shortage of single men however, and in the event, there were slightly more men at the party than women, which was fine with all the women.

The party was in full swing. The guests drifted in throughout the evening, familiar faces had transformed into Shaft, Superfly, Cleopatra Jones and any number of other blaxploitation characters from the seventies. The music also was in the same vein, with the sound system operator sticking, as requested, to the theme of the party. There was music from Sly & The Family Stone, Motown Selections, Stax selections, the soundtrack of the *Car Wash* movie and lots of James Brown, Parliament, Funkadelic, Brass Construction and Hot Chocolate's *You Sexy Thing* and those who remembered how to do it were eager to breathe new life into dances such as 'the bump' and 'the hustle' from yesteryear. There was a cross-section of guests. There were journalists, civil servants, lawyers, advertsing people, accountants, shop managers, nurses, one or two doctors and a few people who seemed to have drifted in uninvited. Some of the guests had come simply to party and were more interested in 'getting down' amongst the other 'wicky wacky people' and others had definitely come to find a partner and who sapent their time out int he conservatory talking, or in the garden, or standing with their backs against the wall in the living room trying to attract the attentions of some of the dancers. And then there were other guests who were there because they had heard that there would be plenty of good food and free drinks all night long. But that was alright for Donna and Dee, everybody was welcome.

By midnight, the ravers were all wet with sweat. Some who couldn't take it, were in a corner sitting down having had as much as they could possibly take. Others refused to leave the dancefloor and started shouting "Here we go, here we go, we go!" as the sound operator teased them with tune after tune that took them back down memory lane to their soul boy/girl days. In-between records, someone shouted out that there was no way they were going to let 'Mr D.J.' go home tonight. The deejay laughed and said, that tonight he was going to "disturb the neighbours" with music they couldn't resist.

Donna was standing in the conservatory, with a broad-shouldered red-skinned man with a shine on his deep-tanned face and who carried himself as if he was somebody important. Tony St Paul looked immaculate and confident enough about himself, behind his dark glasses and Donna could hardly take her eyes off of him. They had danced close together for a full hour in the living room before retreating to the conservatory and Tony had shown himself to be adept at the slow, seductive 'wine'. Whatever record was playing and no matter how fast the rhythm was, Tony stuck to that one, slow, intimate dance which he did so well. He was in his forties, in London on business, and the owner of a group of Jamaican holiday hotels specialising in couples-only resorts.

"Only the Jamaican government employs more people than I do," he boasted above the noise. "All this from having started with a little hotel in Negril which needed renovation... Most things that I put my mind to I end up doing... I've been having a ball all my life."

He confessed that another reason why he was in London was to see if he could find a decent woman for himself, "to powder me every time I come ah England. A woman who knows that there are more than 69 ways to love a black man... a woman who can give me unconditional love and elegant eroticsim."

He raised his eyebrow. Donna continued smiling, wondering whether she should grant him his wish or not. She would be the first to admit that he wasn't exceptionally attractive, but he had so much else to offer. The ball was in her court.

"So," Tony said, "what's a guy got to do to take a woman like you out to dinner some time?"

"You don't have to be perfect," she told him, "you've just got to keep trying."

Dee would rather have been enjoying herself raving, but instead was engaged in a heated argument out in the garden with Roger, a 28-year-old barrister, over the Clarence Thomas issue. He said that whatever had happened between the black Supreme Court judge and Anita Hill, she should have done something about it at the time, not wait until he was about to be elected as the first black judge on the supreme court and then start to destroy his career.

"There are too few black people in those top positions for us to diss them when they reach there. What does that look like to the kids who want role models? It doesn't look too good does it?"

Dee said that that wasn't the issue, it was an issue about a woman who wanted to live her life without being sexually harassed by a guy in a stronger position.

"So many women have to go through that every day in the work place."

Then Roger turned to Robin Givens on his 'bash the women' crusade and the whole Mike Tyson thing. He said he didn't like the way Robin "shafted" the people's champ.

Dee countered that he didn't know anything about what went on between Robin Givens and Mike Tyson in their private lives... It wasn't like Tyson denied it when she told the whole world on prime time television that he was physically abusive to her, even though he was sitting right there beside him.

"And as we can see from the whole Desiree Washington rape episode, Tyson proved to be the kind of man who would do something like that anyway. Women have to be protected from Tyson and all men like him."

Roger insisted that he had watched her testimony in court and just didn't believe her. She must have known what she was doing when she went up to Tyson's room and she must have known that he had a reputation for being insatiable. Why else would he invite her up to his room in the middle of the night —for coffee and cookies?"

Dee was furious. She couldn't believe how backward Roger was.

"Whatever she may or may not have known about Mike Tyson's history, she had every right to go up to his hotel room and not be raped..."

"Okay, okay... maybe we should continue this discussion over dinner one evening," Roger suddenly said out of the blue.

Dee couldn't believe what she had just heard. If this was Roger's way of chatting up women, he would continue being single for a long time to come.

By the time Carol finally braved to come down stairs in hot pants and platform shoes with hooped overknee long socks, it was early morning and there were only about three good looking men left and a number of less desirable ones. There were however, still a number of attractive women and the competition suddenly got stiff for the attentions of men who no one would have given a second thought to earlier. Carol didn't mind though, she had emptied a half bottle of Bacardi upstairs in her room as she built the confidence to come down and when she had had too much to drink all men, even the less attractive ones, seemed highly desirable. Everybody said that they had had a great time at the party, but none enjoyed themselves so much as Carol, who danced the rest of the night away as if she was still seventeen.

MAMA USED TO SAY

Tension had got so tight over Rex Publishing's advert, that the art director and the copy writer began a physical fight right there in the office. I couldn't believe it and went out to mediate. The copywriter had insisted on having his words splashed all over the ad for which they would use a tiny photo, but of course the art director had done the opposite and used the copy really tiny in one corner. I eventually had to overrule. I wanted less copy used and the photo improved if we were going to use it at all.

The launch date for the Rex commercials finally arrived, with 20 huge street billboards in key black areas in London, Birmingham, Manchester, Leeds and Nottingham all featuring the slogan: "Rex Appeal" and with a different black celebrity reading their favourite of the publishing company's books.

Somehow I had been juggling my business life with my personal. Seeing Simon regularly had meant that the one was going into the other.

Simon seemed genuine. We enjoyed each other's company so much that we would be happy going for long Sunday walks together along the river or on Blackheath, just holding hands and talking. We joked and teased each other our lifestyles and our families and our dreams and ambitions and got close to each other over the next few weeks. He said that sometime in his life, he wanted to buy a boat and sail around the world.

"Take a few years off from everything and just sail at

my leisure. It probably won't happen until I'm about sixty and I've been married and had kids who were grown up. But you know, you've got to have your dreams haven't you."

I told him that my dream was to one day have my own magazine.

"It would be something like a 'Lifestyles of the Rich and Famous' for black folk. The magazine would show the private lives of successful black role models with photographs of them at home with their families and that kind of thing. I know a lot of my friends who would buy a magazine like that."

"And I bet it would go down well with advertisers as well," Simon added.

"That's exactly my point."

"Well, what's stopping you from going for it?"

"Money of course. A magazine's going to take time to develop and a lot of cash to get off the ground."

"You should check out Rex Publishing," Simon smiled, "we're always interested in new projects."

"I might just do that," I said.

My mother had always advised that you should judge your men by the way they treat their own mothers, in which case Mamma would have loved this guy. After my first date with him, Simon drove by his mother's house to check up on her. She was living alone in a small flat in Camberwell. She was a youthful looking 60-year-old whose sad eyes brightened up the moment her son let himself in through the front door. She welcomed me in warmly and proceeded to bring out an old family album with photos of her son as a baby."

"He was such a cute child," she explained, "and wherever I took him women would fall in love with him."

"Oh mum, I don't think Dee wants to see those old

photos", Simon said embarrassed.

"My mother is the most important thing in my life," he explained as we drove south to Wimbledon afterwards. "If it wasn't for her I wouldn't be here today. When I think of some of the things that woman has been through to raise her kids, I know that we're never going to be able to pay her back in this lifetime. So me and my brothers and sisters take it in turns to check up on her every evening. Tonight was my turn."

Even though I know exactly what type of man I am looking for, I often seem to experience disappointment. , However, I always had a great time dating Simon. Life was like a big party with him, especially in bed, where it always got pretty hot because my satisfaction was one thing he always took seriously.

For a moment I thought I had found Mr Right, the man of my dreams, who appreciated that I was an attractive and highly sought-after woman (and who also pushes weights to keep myself in trim!)

After a long romantic drought, Simon was just what Doctor Ruth ordered. He had all the right qualities and mixed with all the right people.

I told him straight that I was looking for a 'fine black man'.

"I think you found him," he said with a cheeky smile on his face.

"No I'm not kidding... I'm looking for nothing less than the very best — no compromises."

He said that from what he had heard, African-American men weren't much competition and I had to admit that American men were more concerned about walking around like studs while from what I had seen, English guys seemed to give their women a lot more attention.

With me, it's nearly always 'feast or famine' when it comes to relationships. There are times when more people are interested in me than I can handle and other times when it feels like no one is interested. This was definitely 'feast' time. Simon called me at work and said Andre was in town for a crime writer's symposium and wanted to get in touch with me.

"He wants to know where the most romantic restaurant in London is to take you there."

"That might be a bit embarrassing," I said hesitantly.

I had to explain the situation. That there was nothing going on between Andre and myself and there never had been, but there almost had been and that maybe Andre was thinking that there still could be.

"Does that make sense?"

"No," said Simon laughing. "I bet you just don't want to admit that you've had a fling with him. Come on admit it," he teased.

Joking aside, we still had a problem. If Andre and Simon didn't already share the publisher/writer relationship it might not be so difficult but now...

"Why don't we go on a double date," said Simon. "I'll tell you what you do, invite one of your flatmates along to be my date and I'll come up with some excuse to Andre that it was arranged from time, then everybody's happy. He still gets his romantic evening out with you and you get to have dinner with him, without it becoming compromising in any way."

It sounded like a good idea. I said that I would speak to Donna and Carol and see which one of them wanted to date 'my man' for the evening. Simon laughed and told me not to be jealous and that he'd be keeping an eye on me and Andre the whole evening.

Andre hadn't changed one bit, and as soon as I saw him at the French-African restaurant in Kensington, I started catching those feelings I had previously held for him again. The truth was that I was glad to see someone from back home, but also that I still had a thing for him. Even though the whole set-up seemed awkward I kept my cool.

He said he liked my new hair style. I thanked him without revealing that I had kept the style short, since having had an accident with my curling tongs and burning off half of my hair. I had even grown some feminine sideburns to go with the style, because they were in vogue.

We sat to eat dinner, all four of us — myself, Andre, Simon and Carol. Andre wanted to order the most expensive meals on the menu and the best wine, "or why not some bubbly?"

If Andre had known me better, he wouldn't have taken the liberty of ordering my meal for me, just because he spoke French. I let him sound off for about three minutes, giving the waitress instructions on what I was to have and how it should be cooked.

"Believe me Dee, when you taste this, it will make you fall in love with Moroccan food."

Not if Moroccan food means that you don't respect my independence and judgement, homeboy.

I waited until the food arrived. There were trays and trays of it, meats of every type all neatly arranged in separate plates.

"I'm a vegetarian," I said calmly, looking at the food.

"What?!"

"I don't eat meat."

Andre was embarrassed.

"You didn't give me a chance to tell you..."

He was flustered. His customary self-assured nature had taken a knock, if only temporarily. Fortunately, there were enough vegetables to go with the cous-cous for me to enjoy the meal. I didn't mind and Simon, who had been engaged in a serious conversation with Carol, offered to eat my share of the meat.

"Do you remember that night at the hotel in New York?" Andre whispered. He said he had often thought about it and wondered if the sacrifice of not sleeping with each other had been worth it.

"So how is Shawna?" I asked, reminding him of his commitments, "I know your woman must be longing to see you."

"That's just the point I'm making," he insisted, "I gave up an opportunity to get close to you and I got back to the States to discover that Shawna no longer wanted to get married and had left me. Of all the times to break up... the wedding details were already being arranged and it seemed like my life was more tied to Shawna's than ever before... But it taught me never to depend totally on another person for my happiness."

I told him that I was sorry to hear that things didn't work out with his fiancee, but that I didn't know what all of it had to do with me. He began telling me intimate things about himself that I didn't care to know.

"It's just that you get to a point when you get tired of the bachelor lifestyle — going out meeting beautiful women, and dating. It's time for me to settle down and start a family and have children... I had such a great time with you in New York, at the hotel. I'm too embarrassed to tell you how many times I've thought about that night since... before I go to bed at night... Do you ever think of having kids?"

I was surprised that Andre brought up the subject.

174

Usually men get scared at the very mention of children, seeing kids as an attack on their freedoms. However, touching his desires seemed, I had to make it clear that as far as I was concerned it was too little too late.

"Well I do want kids and a family sometime," I admitted, "but you know what, I'm seeing someone here."

"What a British guy?!" Andre exclaimed.

"Yes, what's wrong with that?"

"Now 'let me get this straight, 25 million black American men aren"t good enough for you home girl?"

I said that there were lots of African-American men who were good enough and even too good for me, but they were all hitched up; as Andre had been previously. What was a poor girl to do? But now I had met a guy and I didn't know where it was all going to go, but I wanted to check it out.

"But we had a thing going Dee, I know what you felt for me and I know what I feel for you. Now I don't know who this other guy is, but you've got to make sure that he's offering you more than I am, that he feels for you as much as I do and that he's gonna love you as much as I will if you give me the chance. Is he willing to have kids with you, just answer me that. If a man's not willing to have kids with you, he's not worth it, believe me."

At this point, Simon who had been deeply engaged in a discussion with Carol, suggested that because dinner was finished maybe we ought to go, as a party, to a private club in Soho, for which he had membership.

Andre finished his drink and 'remembered' that he had an early appointment the next morning. He got up to leave, and looked straight in my eyes.

"Well Dee, I probably won't see you before I go back, but you've got my number in Chicago. The line's always available to you."

175

He said his goodbyes and left the rest of us feeling a bit uncomfortable. The double date had obviously not been a success.

THE REAL MCCOY

When you come out with a winner, you want to go home and tell your friends, "Look at me girl!" But aware that there was always the possibility that things weren't going to work out with Dalton Carol decided there was no point in raising the temperature at home.

"My wife? Oh you must mean my sister," Dalton said when Carol enquired down the phone line.

She had followed Dalton discreetly after work the previous day, just keeping tabs on him. He had jumped into a cab and she had hailed another behind, telling the driver to "follow that cab." At Euston station, Dalton's cab waited as he alighted. He returned a few minutes later with an elegantly dressed black woman on his arm. They had climbed back into the cab and headed West. Carol's driver lost them in the madness of the early evening traffic on Marylebone Road, but she had seen enough and drew her own conclusions. From his description of her, Carol suspected that the woman was Dalton's estranged wife, but he denied it.

"You saw us at Euston? You should have come up and said 'hello'. I've told her all about you. She was down in London for the day from Birmingham and you know, every time she comes down I take her out to dinner at an elegant restaurant. I try to give her a good day out because it's the only break she gets away from her kids."

Dee and Donna weren't convinced. If it was his sister, why hadn't he mentioned her before? And how come his sister who was struggling to bring up three kids as a single mother was dressed so elegantly? Carol knew that her friends were right but she convinced herself otherwise. She had given up too much of herself, too much trust, hopes and feelings to assume the worst. Even if it was his wife, it didn't have to mean much did it? But then again, why couldn't he come clean?

"I was being sneaky checking up on him like that," Carol said, so I've only got myself to blame if he's sneaky back."

The next day Carol went to the hairdressers to have her hair cut in a new short and sexy cut which everybody said took "ten years" off her age. On the way home she stopped by the beauty store and picked up a selection of 'miracle' creams. At home, she waxed her legs for the first time in ages, perfumed her entire body with a fragrance called 'Irresistible' and dressed in nothing but satin underclothes, she lay on her bed for hours, thinking of all the things she had been through then threw an old overcoat on and headed up to Camden.

Dalton was clearly not expecting her, but buzzed her up anyway. The walk up the three flights of stairs seemed to go on forever, every step a reminder to Carol that she could still turn back before making a fool of herself. But no, she had decided to swallow her pride and let Dalton know in no uncertain terms that he already meant so much to her that she would be any woman he wanted her to be, as long as they stayed together.

There would be no embarrassment however, Carol was going to get to keep her coat on. The door to Dalton's apartment was already open when she got there. That was not surprising, it was usually like that once he had buzzed somebody in. She made her way up the next flight within his maisonette, taking her up to the living room, where Dalton was sharing a bottle of wine with a handsome, bronze-skinned man with a handlebar moustache and wearing a sleeveless t-shirt through which his well-oiled muscles bulged.

"You must be Carol," the man said in a lisping soprano, looking the newly-arrived woman up and down. "I'm Darnell, Dalton's 'other half'," he said, giving Dalton a playful squeeze on his thigh. "Thanks for taking care of my boyfriend's 'spiritual' needs whilst I was away. We both appreciate it, don't we Dalton?"

Dalton had been trying to avoid Carol's gaze. He nodded.

At first Carol thought she had misunderstood the man's words. She searched Dalton's eyes for an explanation, but he avoided her gaze.

"Me and Darnell are going through a romantic journey," Dalton said. "The kind of journey you couldn't take me on."

"But..." Carol began, confused.

"I'm a swinger," Dalton explained. "When my wife left, Darnell was there for me when nobody else was."

Carol stood stunned for a moment. There was nothing to say. She felt cheap, used and abused and wanted to cuss Dalton for not telling her before. How could he have allowed her to keep thinking...? How could she have let herself...? But she didn't say anything. After a long while, she turned and went back out the door.

Outside the flat she used a coin to scratch the word 'bastard' across the bonnet of Dalton's beloved Ferrari parked on the street outside.

A week later she registered at Goldsmith's College in New Cross as a mature student. She had forgotten what it was like to be a student, but this second time around, she was determined to enjoy the social life as much as the study. She had decided to do an MA in Law as a refresher course in the subject, before considering going back to Law School afterwards.

She hadn't been at the college long before one of the young black male students called out to her after a meeting of the Afro-Caribbean Society — "Slim body gyal you a look good..." It made her feel secretly good that men who were ten or fifteen years younger found her attractive. Okay maybe they weren't serious, maybe they were just flirting...

If Carol had thought that beginning at college would at least get her off the subject of men and sex and dating, she was mistaken. If anything, she was reminded of her single status even more. At Goldsmith's sex was a hot subject — everyone else at college seemed to be doing it or talking about it.

She had only been at the college for a couple of weeks when one night, to her surprise, the unmistakable figure of her old boyfriend Frankie walked into the bar, recognisable despite the fact that she hadn't seen him for more than ten years. She surprised him by walking up to him and giving him a tight hug.

"Oh Frankie... Frankie?! I just can't believe it. What are you doing here? How are you, how have you been?"

Even though he looked very much himself, somehow Frankie had changed. He wasn't dressed the same way, but in a casual jeans and sweater. He had also mellowed. He was 38, though he could easily pass for 30 now and he seemed mature. She invited him over to her table and they sat and talked over a couple of pints of beer. She thought she had forgotten him, but she hadn't. Sitting opposite him in the smoky student's union bar, she realised that she had lied to herself all this time.

Frankie explained that he was in the final year of an

economics degree at the college. It had hurt him losing his woman because of his reluctance to educate himself all those years ago. And then he had had a daughter with a woman and now his daughter was old enough to come home from school and start asking for help with her school work. Frankie felt embarrassed that one day his daughter would come home from school and he wouldn't be able to explain everything to her anymore. He eventually decided to take his A-levels and so he studied for maths and physics, because he had always been good at and had had an interest in those subjects from school days.

"You were the only person prepared to encourage me at the time and because I could only think of college as selling out, I never appreciated what you were trying to do for me."

He explained also that as a single father it was down to him to bring up his kid, therefore he had to set an example by going through college first, otherwise how could he expect them to follow at some point? Carol was well impressed; was this really Frankie her ex-boyfriend who had refused to read anything — not a book or a newspaper — in the last two years of their relationship? Frankie who was more interested in smoking ganja than in working for a living. She thought of something nice to say about his moustache, which was one of the main ways he had changed. He was still very muscular, so kept up with his training of kung fu she assumed.

First impressions are important. The last thing that Carol was expecting to see was Frankie of all people, with a striped college scarf hanging from his neck and sitting in a student bar somewhere talking about his finals. It made an impression on her and he seemed even more good looking than she remembered him.

He recalled that Carol had decided after university that she deserved somebody else with the same potential as she had, both intellectually and financially... She callously broke off their relationship because he was of lower market value.

Carol was embarrassed by that but Frankie assured her that she had no reason to be.

"I would have done the same thing," he insisted. "You don't realise that when you get a bit of education suddenly the things that meant so much to you before mean so little to you now and you're on a higher level, therefore those around you who have not reached that level become increasingly marginal and you find that you don't have anything to say to them any more and the things you used to do you won't do them no more, and the food you used to eat..."

He asked her how her love life was going, he had heard that she married.

"Great!" she answered without hesitation.

They talked all evening until the bar closed and found out that they still liked talking to each other as much as they had done before and still enjoyed each other's company. While Carol hopped on a train to take her back to Wimbledon, Frankie hopped on a train in the other direction to take him to Elephant and Castle, where he explained he lived with his daughter in a high rise block near Kennington.

Carol promised that she would meet up with him at the college the next day and take him out to a nice little Caribbean restaurant across the road from college where they could get a pretty decent fried chicken, rice and peas and even ackee and saltfish.

EYES ON THE PRIZE

From an early age I saw a lot of deceit in relationships so I decided never to tie the knot with anyone and to just have a string of lovers. Men don't like that kind of attitude in a woman, but I know a lot of other women who have come to the same conclusion..

By the time I was fifteen, I had already stopped believing in love. That was when I fell for Floyd. He was two years older and had left school to start working as a car mechanic and for a girl my age he was seriously cool. I had already had lots of boyfriends but falling in love was a different thing entirely and when Floyd assured me that he felt the same thing, it was easy to give up my virginity to him in one intimate moment. Wendy was my best friend at the time, we had known each other since the juniors. We spent most of our time together, playing netball and sewing raving clothes for each other in my bedroom and trusted each other with all our secrets. Wendy more or less lived round our place, eating there and even sleeping there. She could come by anytime and was like a daughter to my mum. One Sunday her boyfriend Danny came banging on our door after Wendy had gone home asking where she was. She wasn't at home and she wasn't at my house. At that moment, my mum arrived and said she had seen Wendy going into Floyd's house earlier. Danny asked what she could have been doing at Floyd's house. My thoughts exactly. By the time we had walked the few blocks across to Floyd's, Danny had worked himself up so much that he didn't even wait for us to knock, but broke the front door down when we reached. We rushed into the house to find Floyd and Wendy sprawled out on the living room floor, she astride him, groaning and gasping and bouncing up and down as if her life depended on it and he below in a passive role, his hands clasped on her buttocks. I couldn't believe it. Up to this day it hurts bad. The only thing that saved Wendy that day, was Danny who had to pull me off to stop me gouging her eyes out, and the only thing that saved Floyd that day, was me, because Danny had to let him go to restrain me.

Reggie was such a small-minded bastard that he had passed it around that I gave good head and the rumour spread like wild fire. Everywhere I went, I kept coming across people who had heard it and things soon became difficult. Nobody took me seriously when I went for dancing and modelling work. Complete strangers were coming up to me when I went for auditions, making propositions — even women. Shit! I was ashamed. How low can a man go? I had no choice but to keep a low profile and didn't even want to go back to work at Corinna's. Instead I started staying at home a lot more with Carol. Carol loaned me her old sewing machine which had been gathering dust in the attic and I set about making alterations to some of my clothes for want of a better thing to do. That was when Carol suggested that maybe I should try and sell some of those clothes. For the first time in years, I had no interest in men and had enough time to concentrate on what I wanted to do. Never again would I think that the only way I could achieve anything was through a man.

Not every man appreciates a woman who dresses like I do. But then again, not everybody likes dancehall music.

I love dancehall, because that's how I relax. And when I go to dancehall, I like getting dressed up and the more outrageous the clothes the better, because I like to do the opposite of what everyone else is doing and wear the opposite of everyone else. But now it's also my business. I can make money from my creativity. Dancehall doesn't have to be x-rated clothing, just imaginative combinations. I dress to feel good and look sexy. When a man tells me I look sexy, I take it as a compliment, it's not necessarily a come on. Least of all in the dancehall nowadays, where you're gonna see more flesh than fashion. At least amongst the women anyway, who think nothing of wearing a bra, a G-string and mesh stockings just to see who can show the most flesh and get away with it — bare as you dare. Some would say it's unnecessarily explicit, but when all the artists are singing about how your body looks so good, you want to be even more daring.

I dress according to how I feel. But I also dress according to the body I have. I wish I had a body shaped like a coca-cola bottle, but I don't and I'm not putting my body through a lot of emotional stress by dieting, plenty of fruit and vegetables keeps my body healthy. So I've got to get the clothes right. I know I don't have to be a knockout beauty to attract men, all I needed to do was to wear certain clothes like a tiny mini skirt. Yeah, men always go for that, and some lace leggings...

Some women would definitely not look good in the clothes that I wear and design. I wouldn't look good in the ones they wear, but there's something for everyone.

A lot of people consider what I wear as vulgar and men think that you're a sex machine, but that's their business. If you wear hot pants or batty riders and revealing tops or see-through dresses and silk stockings with long gold lame thigh boots, people are going to start saying something.

Even internationally renowned designers are getting into dancehall fashion now. That was Carol's reasoning and if they were making money with our fashions, I couldn't do any worse.

I got paid £50 for my first creation, a red leatherette batty rider with chains on the side, which a friend of Alex's ordered. It wasn't a fortune, but it was a start. The same woman ordered a glittering pussy printer outfit to go with a pair of knee-length suede boots she had just bought. I had to wait a while for word to get around that I could design funky clothes at reasonable prices, but before long I was getting on average of three or four orders a week.

Rap fashions have become every day and who knows with my help, dancehall fashions from the reggae arena could also.

BROTHERMAN

Simon wasn't too happy when I started mentioning kids to him. He said that I had only brought it up because Andre had talked about it at dinner and had wanted to have kids with him.

I said that maybe he was right. Maybe it was Andre's words that had got me brooding, but there it was, I was thinking about kids and couldn't help it. I was a thirty year old woman who was wondering whether it was time to continue the relationship we were having together, whether it would lead somewhere or whether it was going nowhere at all and I might as well just give it up. I told Simon that I wasn't interested in just having an affair that had no purpose, I was too old for that and as much as I enjoyed going out with him, we could continue doing that as friends if anything.

Simon was intelligent enough to know that I was fishing for some kind of declaration of intent. We had been dating each other for several months now. My first anniversary in England was also coming up and although I had a glittering career to show for it, I had a deeper sense of fear of 'missing the boat' than I had in Chicago. I wanted a partner that wanted children. Simon told me that he didn't want to be pressured like that.

I had heard it all before, but it still it hurt me a little that after all we had been through, Simon had the nerve to tell me that he still wanted his freedom, that he didn't want to be hassled, that things were going on fine as they were, why did we have to change it?

"Because I haven't got the time to spend in a relationship that's not going anywhere," I almost screamed at him.

My mood didn't change anything. Simon stopped calling me and I stopped calling him. The relationship, I guessed, was fizzling to nothing.

What was I left with then? I thought about Andre, my next choice. If he was as serious as he said he had been over dinner, perhaps it wouldn't do any harm to call him. I was going to go back home for Christmas anyway and while I was in the States, I was sure that I could make my way over to Chicago even though I didn't have an apartment there anymore.

I rang his number. You know how these things go, I didn't want any more surprises. I wanted him to know in advance that I was coming over and that I was available in as subtle terms as I could muster.

"Hi, how yah doin', I'm sorry you can't get through... just leave your name, and your number and I'll get right back to you," Andre's voice came across the answering machine. Well, that was a good sign. He still lived by himself.

I left as alluring a message as I could.

"Andre sweetie, it's your UK homegirl... just checking up on how you're doing and seeing where you're at and all of that and to let you know that I will be arriving back in the States on Christmas Eve and I will be over for at least a month while I figure out whether I want to go back to work in London or not. You keep promising me dinner at some elegant restaurant in Chicago, so how about it? Call me when you get this message and we can arrange something."

I have no control of my dreams. I wished that all memory of that early evening's dream had disappeared later, but no it was there as clear as day, haunting me. I dreamt that we were making love — me, Donna and Carol — and having toe-curling orgasms. We made love for hours and hours on the conservatory floor and then later because it was a summer's day moved out into the garden to lie in the sun in our bikinis, where we continued hidden from view by the bushes and hedges blocking our garden from the sight of all the neighbouring houses. We had been lying there in the garden caressing for about half an hour, with the radio on at low volume when Donna suddenly started to rub herself all over with a body oil. Before I knew it she was rubbing Carol all over, massaging her. Carol loved it, I felt left out and wanted to be in on it as well. Carol turned and started applying the oil on me and massaging me slowly and sensually. Before I knew it we were exploring each other's intimate parts again and then the orgasms came again, several of them. Donna and Carol both seemed to know exactly what to do to bring me to a climax.

The trouble with dreams is that they never end, but are always interrupted, long before they are over. The sound of the phone ringing brought me out of my deep slumber. I had fallen asleep on the living room rug in front of the fireplace, with the radio on at low volume. I answered the phone. It was Andre.

"Hi..."

He sounded upbeat.

"Dee baby, it was so good to hear your voice again...so how are you doing? Have you married your British guy yet?"

I was embarrassed. Of course that would be one of the things that Andre would want to know, but I hadn't really expected it nevertheless.

"No I haven't actually," I confessed. "All that is over.

We're still good friends, you know, but things didn't quite work out... How about you?"

Andre said that he had some good news. He had just come from Shawna's house and they had ironed out their differences and they had just agreed to fly to Reno the next morning to get married in one of those quickie weddings.

I puffed out a deep sigh, despite myself.

"What's the matter ?" he asked.

"Oh.. nothing, I was just wishing you well... I hope you two are very happy I know how much you care about her."

There wasn't much to say on the phone, I had missed another opportunity to get that ideal man.

WHEEL OF FORTUNE

When black women make it to college, their biggest fear is being turned into a baby mother by their boyfriends? So they leave you in no doubt from the word go that they don't intend to be changing nappies and cooking dinners all their lives. Every single one of those women ended up doing exactly what they swore they'd never do and sidestepped successful careers the moment they started dreading old age at twenty-six, to have babies with sub-standard men.

Frankie told Carol that he had a child on their meeting at college. He said he was now a single father. That his life revolved around his wonderful daughter, six-year old Femi. Things hadn't worked out with her mother, they were still friends, but Jenny now lived in the States with a new man and had left Femi behind in Britain to get the benefit of a good education.

"Traditionally, the single mother gets more stick when it comes to relationships. The minute a man finds out you've got a child, he runs a mile. Men immediately think that you're looking for a father for your child and that you're out to trap them. But fathers too are feeling what its like to be overlooked because they are single parents also, Frankie explained.

"So do you think about getting married again?" he asked her.

By now Carol had confessed that her marriage had been a disaster that she had lived through for seven years, but now she was glad that she was well out of it and able to carry on her own life.

"I do think about marriage but more importantly for my life is to be at peace with myself," she told him.

They were taking a stroll through the park, just talking. Since they had first met at college, they had been seeing each other just on a platonic level, almost learning to know each other again. It had been a bit embarrassing for Carol at first, especially when Frankie teased her about how she had dumped him just because he couldn't get a decent education, but that at the end of the day "God works in mysterious ways" and he wasn't to know then that her getting rough with him would be the cue for him to start studying at some point or other. The way she left him had such an impact on him that he just buckled down and went through the task of going about his O-Levels and A-Levels. Even after Femi was born, he would sneak off to his evening classes just to make sure that he got the degree that everybody, excepting him, seemed to have. And the funny thing was, he added, that since getting the piece of paper, he had begun to behave just like she had done and he no longer could check the type of women he used to check who only seemed to be interested in clothes and raving. The studies had dragged him up to another level. It had been a hard, long slog for a mature student to get through, but he had persevered and it was worth it in the end.

"Don't think that educated and successful women don't get dumped by men as well. I''ve been dumped like everybody else," she said. "Remember the single life that I'm living wasn't out of choice."

Carol couldn't deny that she still had feelings for this man. He was exactly the way she wished he had been ten years ago. She was sure that if he had shown an interest in studying back then they would have had no reason

192

whatsoever to break up.

Was it better to string Frankie along before accepting his advances, or should you seize the magic moment, Carol wondered. When he showed some romantic interest in her she felt like, "No, it can't be true." After all this time he still held a torch for her as she did for him.

She decided still to play hard to get and set about running her quality control checks on him, just to find out if his heart was in the right place.

Frankie said that he wanted a second chance. He was sure that they could make it work this time. Carol didn't disagree but listened,neither encouraging nor discouraging, but wondering whether she was about to choose her mate for the future. But nothing further happened. They were stuck in a romantic stalemate, with each person waiting for the other to make the next move.

Finally Carol sent him a wristwatch accompanied by a perfumed card which read: "I will always have time for you." That was it, there was no holding back now and Frankie quickly responded with his own present, a Zippo lighter inscribed with the legend "Come on baby light my fire."

"We'll start dating," Carol said, "but if you miss one birthday or one anniversary, you pay for it for the rest of our time together..."

Frankie smiled and said that he thought that he could deal with that. That he would give her 100%.

"Why not 150%?" Carol asked,

Frankie really boosted Carol's ego, telling her continually, repeatedly, how much he fancied her and how he couldn't understand how anyone could have left her, or cheated on her. He was the someone she needed who believed in her even when she didn't believe in herself.

Frankie had always been handsome but he seemed to have become more good-looking with time. Some days she would do nothing but gaze at him dreamily when she ran into him between classes at college. That's how good looking he was.

"You're acting like what we did didn't mean anything..." Frankie said.

They had met up in the pub across the road from college, in between classes. It was the day after they had made love for the first time in years. Now Carol was regretting it and wanting to just stay friends.

"I did not go over to your house to make love to you... what was I supposed to do? You wanted to make love as well."

Carol still didn't think it was a good idea. She had sat in her classes all day, wondering what she had let herself in for. Maybe they should have taken much more time before deciding to make love after so long.

Frankie tried unsuccessfully to assure her that everything between them was just like it had been before they made love. They were friends first and foremost and then everything else would develop by itself.

"We've known each other long enough, Carol. I don't have to consider it, I know that you're the woman of my dreams, the woman I've thought about all these years," Frankie said.

Carol listened quietly. She had to admit that she felt the same way as he did. She really didn't have to consider what she thought about him, because it was the same feeling she had when they first met all those years ago and became childhood sweethearts. Like then, her heart told her that being with him was a feeling she couldn't do without.

"At least, let me take you out tonight," he asked her. "I've got a couple of tickets for The Posse down at the Theatre Royal Stratford East, you know that pantomime they do every Christmas — *Pinchy Kobi and The Seven Duppies*. I went last year with Femi and I bought a ticket to surprise her with this years and she said that she would rather go to a friend's birthday party instead."

Carol agreed to meet up with him after college and they would go straight to the theatre and try to talk things through afterwards.

The theatre was packed. *Pinchy Kobi* was a successful and popular production. Carol and Frankie had two of the best seats in the house, right up front by the stage. The side-splitting humour was fast and frenetic. Suddenly in the middle of the pantomime, the rest of the cast stood motionless while Pinchi Kobi walked directly up to Carol in the audience and announced loudly:

"I have been asked by the man on your left, to stop this production and ask whether you will marry him."

At first Carol thought it was part of the pantomime and waited for the punch line. Instead, the spotlight shone on her, and the entire audience fell silent as each and every person realised that this was not part of the show at all.

Almost embarrassed, Carol turned to Frankie. He had a cheeky smile on his face. In front of the entire theatre, he went down on his knees to an affectionate roar of approval from the women gathered there, nudging their partners to ask, "How come you're not that romantic?"

"Answer woman!" Pinchy Kobi shouted, "Answer yes or no, we don't want no maybe... Will you marry this man?"

So many things were going through Carol's mind. Sure she wanted to marry him as soon as her divorce was through. She had wasted the last ten years, it should have been Frankie all along. She didn't need to think about it any longer. The entire theatre roared with approval as she turned to Frankie and nodded enthusiastically. He pulled her close to him and hugged her tight and long.

They were getting on well and Carol found that she didn't need to insist to Frankie that his daughter Femi was always to come first in their relationship. Frankie was a model father and always made sure that Femi was well taken care of anyway. The way he treated his daughter was the way that he might treat a child of theirs if they had one. She had told Frankie about the death of her son Junior, and he had assured her that he had had a blood test for sickle cell anaemia anyway and that he didn't have a trait. Carol was happy and even though it was sometimes inconvenient having to stay around his tiny flat in Elephant & Castle to help him baby sit for his daughter, she didn't complain.

Femi was a lovely girl and she and Carol took to each other immediately. If she had been a complete brat things have been more difficult, but as it was the young girl seemed to know to stay out of the way of her father and his new woman as much as she could and never argued when Frankie told her it was time to go to bed.

Frankie was proof that the caring black father was still alive and well.

"Everybody wants to make out that black fathers are useless and that they are never around when their kids are growing up. I'm here to prove that wrong," he said reassuringly. "I will love you and stay devoted to you and I will be a role model for my children and bring them up together with you in the best way we know how. Not every black man is irresponsible. After all there are a bunch of black men like me with kids by the same woman and with love for their kids."

Carol was suitably impressed. Neville thought that he'd done his bit as soon as Junior was conceived. And that all he had to do after was discipline the child every now and then but otherwise the duty was on the mother's head to make sure the kid ate right and had clothes to go to school with. But Frankie understand that there were other problems in being a black father and that there were things that he would have to teach his children about dealing with life as a black child.

During the next few weeks, Frankie and Carol gave each other as much love and attention as they each needed. They weren't putting on a show, they really did look like the happiest couple in the world, already together for richer or for poorer even though they were not as yet legally married.

"Let's get married African style," Frankie suggested when Carol came by one evening. "We can wait to get the official marriage papers signed when your divorce comes through, but why don't we get married in the ways out ancestors did? And let's do it soon."

Carol was taken aback. She asked what had brought all this about so suddenly? Frankie showed her the opened page in the holiday catalogue.

"I went out today and bought us a honeymoon," he said with a cheeky smile.

Carol read the page hesitantly:

The 'Gold Vacation' it said in the brochure. Fly to the Sandy Lane Hotel in Barbados, where you will be picked up at the airport by a Rolls Royce... with champagne accompanying nearly everything... and including an airplane tour of the island and a ride in a submarine... The cost was only £3,000 per couple.

Carol couldn't believe it. But Frankie's eyes confirmed it, he had done it. He said he had sold a few bits and pieces and that Femi was coming as well. The only thing was that the flights departed on Christmas Eve.

The wedding arrangements were rushed. Frankie already had an idea of what he wanted and discussed it with his bride-to-be and she was agreeable. It would be unusual and interesting and she agreed that the African style ceremony would declare to all who knew them exactly where they were coming from. Carol got Dee to help with the finer details of the ceremony while Donna contributed by getting the material to sew a series of African costumes in the same pattern for all the guests present.

Carol and Frankie were married a few weeks later in the woods of Hampstead Heath before about 70 guests who braved the chill to witness the spiritual, homemade ceremony inspired by African wedding traditions. Their colourful silk outfits, based on royal African wedding clothes, were designed by Carol from original drawings. Frankie was escorted to the ceremony by his 6-year--old daughter, followed by the bride who was accompanied by a banjo player. Before she arrived, several of Carol's female friends formed an aisle for her to walk down. Standing in two parallel lines, they were dressed in identically patterned African women's clothing. As Carol walked between the women, each knelt and placed a small piece of African cloth on the ground for her to step on.

"You're starting a long journey," each one of the women chanted in turn, "may the first steps of your journey be blessed."

As the wind blew through the trees, the couple were

married in a ceremony which they wrote, orchestrated and officiated. They burned sage incense and passed around a conch shell, into which they asked each of the guests to speak into it, as if their words would be trapped like the roar of the ocean forever. Afterwards the guests walked with them to a reception at a hotel. Many sang, carried sunflowers and played drums or tambourines.

Everybody said how much they had enjoyed the ceremony and people went home with their friends and partners grateful for having been witness on a little slice of tradition.

Dee had still not decided whether or not she would return to London after the Christmas. her whole family were bound to be waiting to find out if she had had any romantic success in the UK. It had been something of a disaster in that department. How could she explain to them that whenever true love seemed to be coming over the horizon, it never quite reached her. She leant her head back on the club class head rest and closed her eyes.

"This is your captain speaking, Would the lady in seat 8D please pay attention," the gentleman in seat 10D would like to know whether you will marry him."

Dee listened up like everyone else in the plane at the unusual announcement, not realising that she was in seat 8D. She looked around and saw that all eyes were on her. She glanced at her seat number and then with surprise spun around, to see Simon's smiling face two rows behind her.

NEW!
Black Classics

NEW from The X Press-- an exciting collection of the world's great forgotten black classic novels. Many brilliant black works of writing lie in dusty corners of libraries across the globe. Now thanks to Britain's foremost publisher of black fiction, you can discover some of these fantastic novels. Over the coming months we will be publishing many of these masterpieces which every lover of black fiction will want to collect. The first set of three books are available now!

TRADITION by Charles W Chesnutt

In the years after the American Civil War, a small town in the Deep South struggles to come to terms with the new order. Ex-slaves are now respected doctors, lawyers and powerbrokers–And the white residents don't like it one bit!

A sinister group of white supremacist businessmen see their opportunity to fan the flames of race-hate when a black man is wrongly accused of murdering a white woman. But the black population, proud and determined, strike back.

For a gifted black doctor, the events happening before him pose a huge dilemma. Should he take on the mantle of leading the black struggle in the town, or does his first responsibility lie with his wife and children?

First published in 1901 Charles W. Chesnutt's brilliantly crafted novel is grounded in the events and climate of post slavery America and the white supremacist movement. It graphically captures the mood of the period and is rightly acclaimed as one of the greats of black classic writing.

Black Classics

THE BLACKER THE BERRY
by Wallace Thurman

Emma Lou was born black. Too black for her own comfort and that of her social-climbing wannabe family. Resented by those closest to her, she runs from her small hometown to Los Angeles and then to Harlem of the 1920's, seeking her identity and an escape from the pressures of the black community.
She drifts from one loveless relationship to another in the search for herself and a place in society where prejudice towards her comes not only from whites, but from her own race!

First published in 1929, The Blacker The Berry, caused a storm when it was released. It dared to say what everyone in black America knew, but didn't want to admit. For many years it has remained a lost classic in the vault of black literature but its "raw and penetrating insight" has as much relevance for the black community today, as it did decades ago.

IOLA by Frances E.W. Harper

The beautiful Iola Leroy is duped into slavery after the death of her father but the chaos caused by the bloody American Civil War gives her the chance to snatch her freedom and start the long search for the mother whom she was separated from on the slave trader's block. With the war unfolding around her, Iola endures her hardships with a growing pride in her race. Twice she rejects the advances of a white doctor, who offers to relieve her from the "burden of blackness" by marrying her, and chooses instead to devote herself to the upliftment of her people. It's here that she eventually finds the true love she has been seeking all her life.

Iola was the most widely read black novel of the 19th century and was hugely influential in high-lighting the plight of black American slaves. It was also the first novel which featured a black woman as heroine and was an inspiration for many later black writers.

The
Ragga
& The Royal

WHEN The Princess decides to include inner city problems as part of her charitable work, little does she know where it'll end!

As 'community representative' at a large urban development project, Leroy Massop is about to start working very closely with The Princess on her charitable mission.

They are worlds apart but The Princess is taken by his streetwise charm. Soon a cool working relationship starts to develop into something a lot hotter!

It's an illicit liaison that could destroy the monarchy and her husband, The Prince, is determined that it MUST be stopped. In the meantime Leroy is desperately trying to keep not only his long-term woman sweet, but his 'runnings' as well!

THE HOT NEW BOOK BY **Monica Grant**

Moss Side
MASSIVE

By Karline Smith

"The side of Manchester few people ever get to see...wicked stuff."
VICTOR HEADLEY

"Karline Smith is an author that's certainly going places...She brings an amazing insight and human dimension to crime writing."
THE VOICE

AS baby-faced drug dealers on mountain bikes ply their trade, gun shots shatter the mid-day bustle in Moss Side, Manchester. A young gang leader lies dead on a busy road. No witnesses come forward to help the police.

THE victim's hot-headed brother, now in control of their posse's empire, swears revenge on the boss of a rival gang and his entire family. The score MUST be settled at any cost!

MEANWHILE a mother who once dreamt of 'streets paved with gold', struggles to raise her children alone in Moss Side, unaware of her eldest son's role in the killing and the gangland contract that threatens to destroy everything she lives and works for.

RSVP

Business-Social-Romance

EVERY CONTACT YOU'LL EVER NEED

0839 33 77 20

All calls at 36p per minute cheap rate, 48p per minute all other times.

To record your own free message or reply to one. Tel 071 359 3846

RSVP is Britain's top telephone networking club. For business contacts, romance or socialising, there's no other quite like us. To become a free member write to RSVP, 55 Broadway Market, London E8 4PH. But first check out the messages on the number above.